Amanda's Journey

Amanda's Journey
A DNA Adventure

Ellie Brooks

Amanda's Journey: A DNA Adventure

Copyright © 2022 Ellie Brooks. All rights reserved. No part of this book may be reproduced or retransmitted in any form or by any means without the written permission of the publisher.

Published by Wheatmark®
2030 East Speedway Boulevard, Suite 106
Tucson, Arizona 85719 USA
www.wheatmark.com

ISBN: 978-1-62787-935-4 (paperback)
ISBN: 978-1-62787-936-1 (ebook)
LCCN: 2021925359

Bulk ordering discounts are available through Wheatmark, Inc. For more information, email orders@wheatmark.com or call 1-888-934-0888.

elliebrooksauthor.com
Contact Ellie at elliebrooks.author@gmail.com

*To my supportive husband, Loy,
who helped make this book a reality.*

Chapter 1

◇◇◇◇◇◇

With mixed emotions, Amanda walks up the steps to the Iowa Judicial Branch building. She feels excited about her future yet sad that her first legal job is coming to a close. Her reflection in the glass window brings a broad smile to her face. She likes her new looks; her long hair styled smartly and a new professional-style dress make her feel confident about herself and her future. She strides quickly up the stairs and then pauses, turning to take in the view of the Iowa Capitol complex. Across the street is the five gold-domed statehouse building; it's the only one of its kind in the country. The sweeping staircase on its west side seems to invite the whole of Des Moines to participate in the legislation that occurs within. She will miss seeing this incredible view each day.

She uses the formal, public entrance to the building today. Symbolically, she wants to recreate and remember that first day in 2019 when she walked through the massive brass doors and stepped into the light from the dome onto the breathtaking spiral-designed marble inlaid floor. That day eighteen months ago, when she became the law clerk for Chief Justice Sandra Calhoun.

Typically, a law clerk in Iowa serves for one year starting in August, but Justice Calhoun offered her the opportunity to extend for six extra months, and she jumped at the chance. She has had a great working relationship with her boss, loved the research, preparing summaries, and reviewing opinions for the chief justice. She knew the job was building an excellent resume for her future.

Justice Calhoun helped Amanda with introductions to some of the finest law firms in Des Moines. She contacted her friend, Alan Helling, the managing partner of Helling, Newbiggin, and Sloan, and recommended that he take a serious look at her resume.

It is almost ten o'clock, and she sees Justice Calhoun walking toward her in the Light Court, an atrium courtyard used by court employees for lunch, retirements, and other receptions. But there is no ceremony for Amanda today, just a quiet, personal conversation on her last morning.

As she approaches, Justice Calhoun smiles broadly, "I love your new look, Amanda. Your haircut is terrific, and that dress is perfect for you. The lines of the dress highlight your slim figure. You've created an impeccable image for your new job."

The justice takes a seat, orders coffee, and shares some thoughts with Amanda. "Your new firm is locally known as '*Hell*' not because Helling is the managing partner, but because few prosecutors want to oppose a defense team from Helling, Newbiggin, and Sloan; perhaps because they are always well-prepared. Helling hires the best of the best, and you fit that category. You can expect to be managed by a partner; his clients will become part of your responsibility. You will mainly do research and write briefs. It will be demanding, especially in your first year as a neophyte associate. You should expect high demands for billable hours. The senior partners are great rainmakers; they know all the state's important political and business people. Once they've secured the client, the partners expect the firm's lawyers to put forth long hours to generate profits for the firm and its owners. Amanda, remember it's all about profits. This demand for action also contributes to their being called 'Hell.'" So, it won't be easy, and you'll have scrutiny of your work in the first year, but I am confident you will be successful in their environment and will be one of their new shining stars.

"Thank you for all your wonderful research and writing these last eighteen months. You were always well-prepared, and your research was impeccable. In addition, you're an organized, intelligent, and punctual person, all attributes I value. You've set a standard for the other law clerks in this building and your replacement," Justice Calhoun's friendly smile reaches her eyes. "I will miss working with you and hope we can have lunch after you get settled at your new job. I'd like to stay in touch as you rise through the judicial system in Iowa. Who knows, possibly someday you'll have my job."

Amanda shakes her head, "Justice Calhoun, your job is not on my radar screen. I know how difficult it can be, and I'm not aspiring to take on that level of responsibility. Maybe I'll change my mind in thirty years, but right now, it's intimidating even to think about considering a future justice position."

"Amanda, whatever happened in your relentless search for your birth parents? Last time we talked, you were leaving for St. Cloud, Minnesota, to see if you could find your original birth certificate or any helpful leads."

"Guess I've been a better law clerk than a genealogy detective. I found nothing, or as they say at the ballpark, I struck out. The courthouse clerk knew I was a lawyer. She graciously allowed me to review the birth records; there was a set of twin girls and three boys born on my birthdate. There was no record of me. I visited one of the older nurses at the hospital, and she shared that it wasn't uncommon for nurses to change information on the records when they knew someone was adopting the child. It was just a slight change that would throw others off. She said they might change a birth date to the week before or after to protect the birth mothers and their families. She even gave me the name of an old nurse who worked at the hospital when I was born; I found her living in an assisted living facility. She confirmed that she had changed records many times for babies taken from the mother just moments after birth. Based on her confession, I checked back with the courthouse, but even a week before or a week after my birth date revealed only two female birth certificates. I followed up on both and found them living in St. Cloud. As you suggested, I went to the local social services agency, and they had no record of adoption for anyone born on or near my birthdate. I'm at a dead-end; I have to accept that I may never discover the truth about my birth parents. But I appreciate all your suggestions; you gave me the right direction, but there was no evidence there to help me."

"I'm sorry, but sometimes that is the case. Adopted children want to find closure. Identifying their birth parents provides closure; they hope to understand why their biological families did not keep them. But the laws are changing, and opening up records is becoming more common. So don't give up."

"Justice Calhoun, thank you for all you've done for me. I can't tell you how much I've learned under your leadership and direction. I will call and get a luncheon date on your calendar in a few weeks. Thanks for all your direction and advice."

The justice stands as a signal that their time together is over. She walks over to Amanda, gives her a warm hug, and whispers, "Go get 'em, girl!"

Amanda leaves the building, wrapping her winter coat tightly around her in this cool, windy February weather. She walks quickly down the path to James Ellwanger's fantastic thirty-foot sculpture, *Shattering Silence*. The circular band on the sculpture's interior holds sixteen flat metal shards that jettison out in all directions. She recalls that it commemorated an 1839 Iowa Territorial ruling when Iowans refused to stand by silently when they saw injustice. Amanda runs her hand over the smooth sides of one of the metal shards. She turns and pauses to ponder her future as she looks west at the panoramic view of the skyline of downtown Des Moines.

Chapter 2

Amanda is excited. It's her first day in her chosen profession. She's finally going to practice law as a defense attorney for real clients and cases. She quickly walks through the lobby of the Ruan Center, smiling at the security guard as she passes to the elevators for the ride up to the 23rd floor.

Stepping off of the elevator, she approaches the receptionist. She extends a warm smile that reflects brightly in her eyes. Noticing the nameplate, she greets the attractive woman behind the desk. "Good morning, Ms. Olsen. My name is Amanda Springs. Today is my first day with the firm. Can you direct me to the Human Resources Manager?"

"Welcome to the firm, Ms. Springs." Nodding toward the woman sitting beside her, "This is Mary from HR. She will escort you to the conference room. We've been awaiting your arrival." Mary extends greetings and takes Amanda down the staircase to the conference room on the 22nd floor.

Mary introduces Amanda to her new colleagues: Aaron Sloan-Brown, Kathyrn Baker, and Christopher Reed. Amanda checks her watch, worried that she had been holding up the start of the meeting. Seeing that she's fifteen minutes early, she realizes they must be as excited as she is to start their new law careers.

Day one at Helling, Newbiggin, and Sloan is a day full of orientation. Human Resources is the first on tap for the four newly hired attorneys. They sit along one side of the conference table, filling out the requisite employment documents while the HR specialist outlines their rights, responsibilities, and obligations. The firm's experts come into the room, sitting on the opposite side of the table, to explain the various documents. Next to arrive is a Benefits Specialist; she describes the choices available for the health care and dental benefits; they each complete the forms selecting their desired options. This process goes on throughout the morning with a new presenter every half hour. The Benefits Specialist distributed the employee handbook explaining key elements. She admonishes them to read the entire manual within the first week and bring the signed acknowledgment form to the human resources office.

Before noon, the HR Manager comes into the room, introduces herself, and hands each of them a confidential envelope. The contents outline compensation, vacation and personal days, bonus opportunities; in short, all the things they individually negotiated before accepting the offered position as a new associate in the Helling firm.

The four new lawyers were treated to a box lunch and were left alone to get acquainted. Aaron Sloan-Brown starts the conversation with an abrupt, inappropriate question, "Okay, what are they going to pay you? Are we all in the same ballpark?" Christopher Reed rolls his eyes and looks down the table at Amanda, who looks dumbfoundedly at Aaron.

Amanda sighs and confronts her new colleague, "Aaron, you'll find that I'm a direct person; you never have to guess where I stand on an issue. I won't mince words when I say that's an inappropriate question. When you read the employee handbook, one of the cardinal rules will be you never talk about your salary with your co-workers. I could be wrong about the manual, but what I negotiated based on my education, background, and experience is private between the firm and me."

Christopher says, "Well, I agree one hundred percent with Ms. Springs. But I don't mind sharing that I'm getting a million and a half as a starting salary." Aaron's mouth drops to the table before he realizes that Christopher is jerking his chain. "Okay, it's lower than that, but Amanda's right; the terms of my starting salary and bonus arrangements, if any, are private." Kathryn nods her head in agreement, her eyes moving quickly from one to the other; she finally lowers her eyes and becomes fixated on eating her salad.

"Wow, an attorney who doesn't like controversy," Amanda thinks to herself. "Kathryn, what area of the law interests you the most?" She looks at Amanda on her right, smiles in relief that the previous conflict is over. She explains she has her JD degree, a master in business and accounting, and is excited to be an attorney in the tax department. "I love working with business finances, and hopefully, someday, I'll have a chance to work on international money laundering."

Before she could ask the same question of Christopher and Aaron, the conference room door opens, and the caterer clears away the luncheon debris and sets the room with fresh water and beverages. Once the room is clean and orderly, the HR Manager returns with the agenda for the balance of the day.

"Next, you will have a tour of the 23rd and 22nd floors of the Helling offices. The law library will be your first stop. There the librarian will assign use instructions and access codes for the digital files. After a quick tour of the main lobby, the executive conference rooms, and offices of the senior partners on the 23rd floor, we will come back down here, where our employees accomplish most of the real work." She chuckles at her humor.

"Additional topics for this afternoon include mundane but important how-tos. First and most important, how to track your billable hours and complete the biweekly timesheets." Amanda mentally recalls Justice Calhoun's remarks, "it's all about profits."

"Finally, your supervising partner will be waiting to give you their specific instructions, make some initial case assignments and then take you to your newly assigned office or workspace. If you are assigned an assistant, your supervising partner will make the introductions. New business cellphones and laptops will be waiting for you on your desk. For the balance of the day, you are free to get settled into your office. Any questions on the goals for the afternoon?" All four heads shake simultaneously in the negative.

Just at that moment, as though timed precisely, the door to the conference room opens. "This is Carol Summers; she'll be your guide for the afternoon tour. Again welcome to the firm; I look forward to getting to know each of you in the weeks and months ahead. Stop by our department if you have questions or need help." She turns to leave as Carol invites everyone to follow her.

Before leaving the conference room, Christopher suggests, "How about the four of us meet for a glass of wine to celebrate our first day." Nods of agreement all around, "Okay, let's plan on meeting at the Renaissance Savery lobby bar at five forty-five." They were out the door for their afternoon tour.

The four new attorneys arrived promptly at five forty-five at the lobby bar named Cøda. They find two facing sofas in a quiet corner near the window; a coffee table is between them. They each order their favorite glass of wine.

Aaron begins the conversation, "Okay, what's your first impression, who's your supervisor, where's your office, and tell one personal thing about yourself."

Kathryn offers to go first, "I am impressed with the on-boarding process of the firm. I think the HR professionals have a thorough and effective process to bring on new attorneys. I'm thrilled to be a member of the team. The tax partner, Dick Jones, is my supervisor, and I think we clicked. My office is on the 22nd floor in the cubicles, near the staircase coming down from the 23rd floor. Aaron suggests we share a personal item from our lives." she pauses, "I was born in Ireland, and an American family adopted me. How about you, Aaron?"

"Really! You were born in Ireland. Shouldn't your last name be O'Baker?" Aaron chuckles. Kathryn rolls her eyes at his attempted humor as Aaron continues. "I've been assigned to accidents and injuries. Jane Carroll is my supervisor, and like Kathryn, my cubicle is near the main staircase to the 23rd floor. I am happy to have been hired; I didn't think I had a chance as many law classmates applied to this firm. This spring, I will graduate from Drake University Law School. I will work on research until I pass the bar. As a personal item: I get to study for the bar during the business day."

Taking a sip of his wine, Christopher smiles at Aaron. "Congratulations, Aaron. It sounds like you've negotiated a perfect deal. If you need help studying for the bar, give me a shout; been there, done that, and I can share my experience. I've been working as a teaching assistant at Drake University and waiting for an offer from a good quality firm. I believe we all have been hired by the best. Amanda and I are both delighted to use our skills in Davis III's business litigations department. Our offices are back on the west wall of the 22nd floor. We share an assistant. Finally, I grew up in Minnesota, and I'm a reasonably good golfer; I've been playing since I was eight."

Aaron interrupts, "An assistant, you two have an assistant? Wow, I'm envious. Guess I will have to learn how to use all the copy machine codes they taught us today. It sounds like you'll have someone to do that for you."

Amanda sighs, "Don't jump to any conclusions, Aaron. I'm guessing we will see a lot of each other at the copy machine. As for me, I echo what you all have all said. I'm thrilled to be a team member in *Hell*. The firm is one of the best in the city and probably the state. I'm a graduate of the University of Iowa Law School. I spent the last eighteen months as a law clerk for an Iowa Supreme Court Justice. I was impressed each time I heard an attorney from this firm argue before the seven Supreme Court Justices; their preparation, legal knowledge, and communication skills were head and shoulders above other lawyers. I think we all scored."

Amanda raises her glass, "May I offer a toast to my new colleagues? Here's to good times and hopes that we all get through the probationary period with flying colors."

"Hear, Hear." They clink their glasses, and Kathryn stands to leave, claiming a prior commitment. Aaron says he's off to study and will see us in the morning.

Christopher and Amanda linger over their glasses of wine, order an appetizer, a second glass and continue their conversation. Amanda breaks the ice, "I can't believe how lucky we are to be working for Davis III. I look forward to working with you." She raises her glass to the handsome man sitting just inches away from her and wonders if he can hear the fast beat of her heart. She's upset with her reaction to his physical presence. This instant attraction has never happened to her before. She feels her attraction to him and wonders if he senses how off-balanced she feels.

Amanda asks about his family. Christopher shares, "My parents own a well-known custom cabinet business in the Twin Cities area. It's a family-owned business that spans three generations of Reed ownership. I've worked with my dad during the summers, both in high school and college, but I never enjoyed the dusty hands-on work of constructing expensive cabinets for new homes. It has never been my passion like it is for my dad and brother. Dad hoped I would follow in his footsteps and someday run the company. He didn't argue when I decided to go to law school, as he felt it would be great to have an in-house lawyer. I didn't tell him that wasn't my plan."

Amanda inquires, "The University of Minnesota has a wonderful law school; why didn't you go there?"

"I decided to leave Minnesota and go to Drake

University because I liked the idea of smaller classes, direct access to the professors, and, frankly, being on my own a few hundred miles away from home. I grew to like this city and its opportunities. I decided to stay and start my career here. I love Des Moines' brand marketing slogan, *'the s's are silent; but the place is a buzzin.'* It exactly describes how I feel living here. Dad still has hopes that I will reconsider and return to Minneapolis."

"Sounds to me like you are walking away from a great opportunity. You could have had a guaranteed job for life. Assuming, of course, you have the grit required to run a successful business like your dad," she chuckles.

"Okay, okay, smarty. Yes, you are right; and I can always change my mind. But I would like to be successful first on my own merits, talents, and hard work, not because I'm the boss' son. What about you, Amanda?"

"My life is not quite as interesting as yours, but I'm proud of my family and the opportunities they made available for me. I grew up in Pella, just fifty minutes to the east of here. But unlike you, I don't know even one generation of my family, let alone three. Like Kathryn, I am an adoptee. My biological parents and grandparents, aunts, uncles, and cousins are all unknown to me."

"I am sure there is an appropriate response to what you've just shared, but I'm not sure what it would be. To my knowledge, I've never talked with an adopted person. How did it make you feel when you learned your parents adopted you and they were not your biological parents?"

"I've always known I was adopted or as my parents would say '*I was not expected but was selected.*' When I was a little girl, my mother would read bedtime stories about adopted children. She made me feel that I was something special. I never had the feeling of loss or abandonment that other adoptees claim to have experienced. I was their little girl, and I received the same love and support that my brothers, who were their natural children, received. They are great parents, and I will always appreciate everything they've done for me.

"As you can tell, I feel very fortunate to have been selected to be part of the Springs family. Nothing was ever uncomfortable or unsettling for me, but I don't know how to say this," she pauses, trying to find the right words, "I do feel a need to fill a void created by the unknown. I would like to know who my biological parents were and why they gave me up. Knowing might allow me to feel whole or satisfied, or whatever the right word is. It is not like I think about it every day, but I have an ongoing yearning to discover the truth."

Catching a glance at her watch, "Christopher, It's almost eight o'clock." She is shocked at how quickly time has passed. "I need to head home for the evening. I plan to read the employee handbook and turn in my signed acknowledgment form tomorrow. I want to get all this start-up stuff off my plate and do some real work." Dropping a few bills on the table, she rises to leave. "That should cover my drinks and half the appetizers. I'll see you bright and early in the morning. Thanks for suggesting this get-together. I've enjoyed it."

"Amanda, I've enjoyed getting to know you. By the way, do you like Starbucks coffee?"

"Yes, I do; why?"

"I have a routine of stopping at Starbucks to get my day started. I'll bring you a cup of java in the morning. Enjoy reading your boring handbook. I'll see you tomorrow."

Amanda walks out of the lobby bar as Christopher enjoys the view of her slim, shapely figure. In his mind, he is trying to sort out his feelings for Amanda; he's never been more attracted to a woman in his life.

Chapter 3

◇◇◇◇◇◇

It's day two at the law office. Amanda arrives early. She worked hard for a couple of hours on the cases assigned to her yesterday. There is a scheduled staff meeting at nine-thirty. Christopher comes in at nine o'clock with Starbucks coffee and scones for both of them. "Are you just arriving for the day? I thought you stopped at Starbucks on your way into work," she smiles with humor in her eyes.

"I've been in the law library since six. I made a special trip to Starbucks, just for you," he playfully responds. They continued chatting, giving each other flirtatious looks that were evident to both.

"Christopher, I enjoyed the Savery last night, particularly after Kathryn and Aaron left. I feel like we are more mature in some strange way. Unlike Kathryn and Aaron, we both passed the bar a year or two ago, and we've had outside experiences before joining the firm. I hope we can be friends on and off the job."

"I agree, Amanda. But did you see the employee handbook warning that the firm frowns on intra-firm relationships? If it's a relationship between a boss and a subordinate, it's strictly verboten. Lucky for you, I'm not your boss because I'm interested in getting to know you."

"Lucky for you, I'm not your boss." Amanda teases back.

As they leave her office for the staff meeting, Christopher sees Aaron ahead on the stairs. He leans in and quietly asks, "Did you hear my side conversation with Aaron last night?"

"Not that I can remember."

"He's the grandson of one of the founders of the firm, Milton Oliver Sloan. That explains why the firm hired him before he passed the bar."

"Shez! Really! Good to know."

Amanda is impressed with her surroundings as they walk down the posh hallway on the 23rd floor with its fine art, wainscoting, and luxurious carpet. Certainly nothing like the sleek marble and beautiful brass décor of the Iowa Judicial Building. "Smells and feels successful, don't you think?" she whispers to Christopher.

In the staff meeting, the managing partner announces that Amanda and Christopher are assigned to work together on an embezzlement case involving the daughter of a politically important firm client. It is news to them, and they look at each other with excitement in their eyes.

They leave the staff meeting with R. Jordan Davis III and head to his office. Davis III outlines the details of the case. "You will only be doing the background and legal research; I will be representing the client at the defense table. As was announced at the staff meeting, it's an embezzlement case. The accused is a thirty-eight-year-old female named Darla Wilson. She is the daughter of a powerful local politician, J. Gifford Wilson, who lobbies for the firm on legislative matters. I would like you to set up a meeting with Ms. Wilson and prepare a brief outlining the facts from her viewpoint. She was the bookkeeper for Lark Monahan, the owner of Lark Chevrolet in West Des Moines. He accused her of embezzling more than $97,000. After visiting with Darla, please schedule time on my calendar to brief me on your findings. Hopefully, you can get this first step completed within the next ten days."

He emphasizes that this case takes priority over their other billable work. "The judge has called for a pretrial conference to set a calendar for this case. You will attend the pretrial conference with me, add the date to your calendar; the judge will hold the meeting three weeks from this Friday."

As they walk down the sweeping staircase together, Amanda sees Kathryn in her cubicle and gives her a warm smile and a wave. Turning to Christopher, "She does have a great view of who is coming and going between the floors. But as a tax attorney, I'm sure she'd like a quieter place to concentrate; we will have to tell her about the small workroom on our end of the floor."

Before they reach the bottom step, Aaron jumps out of his cubicle and quickly approaches them. "Hey, you guys, how lucky can you get an embezzlement case as your first assignment? It should be a fascinating case, and you'll get to work closely together.

"By the way, I saw your offices on the other end of the floor. I'm impressed, locking glass doors, floor-to-ceiling windows, and an assistant outside your office. Is there an adjoining door between your offices, too?"

"Wow, Aaron," Christopher replies, "sounds like you are a little green with envy. Wait until you pass the bar; I'm sure the grandson of a founding partner will get an even better office in the future." Without waiting for a reply, Christopher continues walking down the hallway to his office.

Startled by Christopher's sudden departure, Amanda searches for something to say. After a somewhat lengthy pause, she asks, "How is the studying going, Aaron?"

"Just fine, thanks for asking."

"Great, have a good day, Aaron. See you later." She heads to her office to read and digest the police report and the district attorney's charges on the embezzlement case.

After eating lunch at her desk, Amanda goes to the law library at one o'clock to meet Christopher. They begin by reviewing the contents of the district attorney's case. "Our client Darla Wilson is facing a first-degree theft charge that could result in a ten-year prison term," Christopher begins.

"Powerful Daddy is not going to want to see that happen," Amanda suggests.

Christopher reading from the file summarizes the case. "According to the police report, Lark Monahan at Lark Chevrolet hired Darla to handle the bookkeeping and be a watchdog on expenses. Monahan states in the police report that he was initially delighted with her work, but he became concerned when vendors started complaining about late payments of their invoices. When he discovered Darla had not paid the parts invoice to General Motors, he panicked about his dealership's reputation. He contacted his CPA and requested an unannounced audit. The CPA discovered the embezzlement, and Lark filed a police report.

"The prosecuting attorney claims Ms. Wilson embezzled the money through an elaborate scheme of fraud. The CPA discovered that several copies of cashed checks were missing from Larkin's files. When he compared the items to the bank statement images, he found all the missing checks had been made payable to and cashed by Darla Wilson."

"Christopher, the prosecutor's case sounds convincing, but we both know we need to hear the other side of the story, Darla's story. Then we have to create a strategy to defend her in court." They accessed their electronic calendars to find a mutually acceptable date for the first discussion with Darla. Amanda agrees to make the call to invite her to the office.

"Let's make a list of the questions to ask Darla." Amanda accesses the whiteboard and starts writing a list of questions.

Christopher and Amanda continued brainstorming until they had filled the whiteboard with questions. "Have you used a smart whiteboard before?" Christopher inquires.

"No, I haven't," Amanda admits.

"Watch this" He taps a stylus on a question and drags it to the bottom of the whiteboard. "We just move the questions around until we have them in a logical order." With the prioritization complete, Christopher saves the image to his laptop, sends a copy to be printed, forwards a copy to Amanda's email, and then erases the electronic whiteboard with the click of a button. "This is cool technology and exceptionally productive. When you get back to your office, Amanda, you will have both the image I just erased and a text document waiting in your email. I'll stop by the printer and pick up the hard copies."

"Christopher, I'm impressed with your technical skills. Where did you learn how to operate it?" Amanda sends him a smile of admiration.

"We used the same whiteboard at Drake. I taught a class for first-year law students, so I'm familiar with it."

"Just saying, you're impressive." she gives him a broad warm smile.

Amanda returns briefly to her office and calls Darla to set up a meeting. She dials, expecting that she will have to leave a voice message. To her surprise, Darla answers the phone. "Good afternoon, my name is Amanda Springs with the Helling, Newbiggin, and Sloan law firm. I'd like to speak with Darla Wilson."

"This is Darla."

"Ms. Wilson, my colleague, Christopher Reed, and I have been assigned to work with your attorney, R. Jordan Davis III, on the charges of embezzlement that the district attorney has filed against you. We need to meet with you at our office to hear and understand your side of this—"

Darla interrupts and loudly, with extreme anger, states, "Well, I can tell you this is bullshit. It's Lark Monahan that the district attorney ought to charge with fraud. He's trying to throw me under the bus and ruin my career. He's doing it to save his ass."

Calmingly, Amanda replies, "that's why we want to talk with you. There are always two sides to every story, and we need to hear what you know and why you feel the prosecutor filed these charges. Would you be available to come to our office on Thursday morning at ten o'clock?" Darla agrees to the time and date. "It will probably take a couple of hours. When you arrive, go to the main lobby on the twenty-third floor of the Ruan Center, and they will direct you. We'll see you on Thursday."

Amanda heads back to the law library, smiles, and gives Christopher a high-five. "We are on. She will be here on Thursday at ten."

Christopher suggests they get a quick bite to eat

around six o'clock and then return to the office for more research on prior embezzlement cases. They leave the law library and return to their offices to make phone calls and complete work on other pending legal files. Amanda prepares a summary of the day's findings, including the first meeting date with the client, and sends a text to Christopher to check the shared computer drive for the document. She wants him to review it before she sends an electronic copy to Davis III.

As Amanda is getting ready to leave the office, the phone rings. She answers with her usual greetings.

"Amanda, my name is Tom Graves. I'm an attorney in Iowa City. I will be in Des Moines tomorrow and would like to meet with you if you're available."

"Tom, we've never met. May I ask what this is about."

"It is a private matter that I would like to discuss in person over lunch." She's confused by his request but agrees to meet the next day. She adds the appointment to her calendar for noon with Tom Graves at the Court Avenue Brewery and wonders, "I wonder what's this is about?"

Christopher and Amanda leave the office and chat as they walk to Centro, one of the most popular downtown restaurants. As the hostess escorts them to their table, they frequently stop to greet people they know. Amanda chats with a former colleague, as Aaron Sloan-Brown brushes by Christoper. Seeing Amanda, he nudges Christopher, "So what's happenin' buddy?

Are you making it with your embezzlement case colleague?" Christopher does not reply but gives him a look of abject disgust. Aaron proceeds to a table in a back corner with an air of importance where three attorneys from Hell's accident and injury department are having cocktails.

When Amanda joins him at the table, he draws Aaron to her attention. Christopher admits that Aaron is quickly becoming an annoying co-worker.

Chapter 4

◇◇◇◇◇◇◇

Amanda arrives at the office, continuing the habit she established at the Supreme Court; her goal is to be the first lawyer in the office each morning. Christopher is in his office already. He gets up from behind his desk with a massive smile on his face. He follows her to her office with a cup of her favorite Starbucks in his hand. She realizes that there's going to be some competition now as to who arrives first. They share morning greetings; he sits across from her desk as they drink their coffee and establish what will become a morning routine. "Let's meet later this afternoon for an update on the status of our case," he suggests, standing up as he gets ready to leave. "It's time for me to get back to my office and generate more billable hours." It appeared he was contemplating whether to say something more, but no words escaped his lips. They were suspended in time, staring into each other's eyes. With a smile on his lips, he backed his way to the door. "It's been a pleasure to see you this morning, Ms. Springs." She smiles and laughs.

Amanda works all morning, handling calls, scheduling clients, giving instructions to her assistant, and working on the embezzlement case. She leaves for her scheduled luncheon with Tom Graves and walks through the skywalk to Court Avenue at eleven-thirty. She loves the city skywalk system; she never has to wear a winter coat, and regardless of the weather, you can reach most restaurants, shopping, and business locations without going outside.

Precisely at noon, she arrives at the Court Avenue Brewing Company; he's waiting for her at the hostess stand. Reaching out his hand, "You must be Amanda Springs. I'm Tom Graves."

"Yes, I am, but how did you know?"

He hands her a photo of herself, a newspaper article from eighteen months ago announcing her appointment as a law clerk for Justice Sandra Calhoun. "You haven't changed much."

"Do you always scope out information about people you are meeting for the first time?"

"No, no," Tom assures her. Amanda realizes that she needs to hold her questions until they are safely secure in the privacy of a booth.

After the waiter took their order, Tom began to tell her the purpose of his visit. "I'm the family attorney for Bob and Mary Anne Myers." Handing her a newspaper clipping from *Iowa City Press-Citizen* (Iowa City, Iowa) dated September 23, 2019, he continued. "They were killed in an accident when a drunk driver hit their car. It was a senseless death caused by a drunk driver going the wrong way on Interstate 80 east of Iowa City."

Amanda shares, "I remember seeing the report of this accident on television and reading about it in the newspaper. I also remember there were several legislative bills against drunk driving that ensued and were circulating in the Iowa Statehouse."

"I have been the Myers' attorney for the last sixteen years; shortly after they were married, they hired me to draft their wills. My wife, Jill, is..." he pauses, "was one of MaryAnne's closest friends. We liked them the minute we met, and Jill and I spent a great deal of time with them socially. We were together every weekend, either in each other's homes, at university sporting events, or having celebration dinners at gourmet restaurants for birthdays and anniversaries. It's their will that brings me to you today."

Amanda's face expresses her continued confusion. "Tom, I'm sorry if there's been some misunderstanding, but I don't handle accident and injury cases, nor do I specialize in wills and trusts. We have many fine attorneys in our firm that might have a better legal background on these topics. Now that I think about it, why are you looking for an attorney when you are one?"

"No, there has been no misunderstanding; this

isn't about needing legal advice, Amanda. You and your twin sister are beneficiaries named in their last will. They were your birth parents." Amanda doesn't realize that her jaw has dropped open, and she is staring at him as though shell-shocked. She is speechless. His comment that he wanted to discuss 'a personal matter' meant that it was *personal* to her.

Amanda is both stunned and intrigued to learn more. Suddenly, the questions spill out non-stop, "*What*? I have a twin sister? How did my birth parents get this newspaper story about me? How did they find me? How did they know I was the daughter they put up for adoption? Why haven't they contacted me? I've been looking for—" She realizes she's babbling and falls silent, dropping her hands into her lap. Her mind is reeling, and her heart is a race car. "Tom, I don't even know these people. Why would they think I'm their daughter? Are you sure this is true?"

"Yes, Amanda, I know that it is true, and before they died, they knew all about you. They followed your successes through law school, attended your graduation, and were proud when you were selected to be a law clerk for the Iowa Supreme Court." Amanda slumps back into the booth; she is awestruck.

"Bob and MaryAnne were high school sweethearts in Marshalltown, Iowa. They met during her freshman year when he was a sophomore. They were always together, and everyone who was a friend of theirs knew they were soulmates and would stay together. Their friends saw them as a perfect couple and dreamed they would go to college together, marry and live happily ever after. But then MaryAnne became pregnant in her sophomore year.

"Once they learned about the pregnancy, Bob's 'old-school victorian' father, George Myers, refused to allow him to marry. Bob's dad did not consider her worthy of his son. As far as he was concerned, she was not in his socio-economic class. None of Bob's pleas that he loved MaryAnne and could be responsible for the child persuaded his father to change his mind. Marriage was out of the question; he was a minor, and his father legally had the right to make this decision with or without his agreement. The family attorney was present during these heated discussions and explained the options.

"MaryAnne's parents were Jon and Gabriella Blanc. They agreed with George Myers, probably because they weren't financially in a position to help the young couple or fight for their daughter's reputation. George Myers certainly made it clear he wouldn't help or support them. He insisted they give their baby to willing adoptive parents; he would handle all the legal arrangements. George would not allow his son to ruin his life or the remaining two years of his high school basketball career. He still had college in his future, and he couldn't be successful if he supported a wife and baby at age seventeen. His father reminded him that he should have thought of that before he had unprotected sex. His father, by the way, was one of the most popular and successful obstetricians in central Iowa.

I'm sure he delivered a few children born out of wedlock and probably used that same line with a few of his patients.

"MaryAnne was sent to live with her mother's sister, Aunt Clara, in St. Cloud, Minnesota. During this period, Bob did not know where she was living and had no contact with her. He did as was demanded by his father, and eventually, he stopped looking for MaryAnne and got on with his life. When the time came for the baby's delivery, her mother, Gabriella Blanc, and Bob's mother, Toni, went to Minnesota. Gabriella made the trip to be with her daughter, and Toni was in charge of bringing the baby back to Marshalltown for the private adoption process."

"But you said I was born a twin." Amanda's forehead wrinkles with her confusion.

"Yes, that fact became known only at the time of the birth. It wasn't one baby, but two; MaryAnne had twin girls." Amanda has tears in her eyes as she continues listening intently to the history of her early days after birth.

"Your adoptive parents were over the moon with excitement when they heard you had been born; within two days, you were in their arms, and a few weeks later, the attorney finalized everything. MaryAnne and her parents signed away all legal rights to handle the adoption to the 'good' Dr. George Myers, who had convinced them he was in the best position to handle the adoption matter. George never told your adoptive parents about the twin sister. Without caring, he took your twin to the Des Moines Social Services and put her up for adoption.

"Once the agency placed your twin sister with her adoptive family, she was lost to you and the family. Efforts to find her were unsuccessful, and her adoptive surname is not known. MaryAnne named the babies Emily and Emma at birth. But Emily's name was changed after the private adoption when a new birth certificate was issued. Emily became Amanda Emily Springs."

Amanda places her hand over her mouth as tears glisten in her eyes. She realizes the kind gesture of her adoptive father and mother. They had kept a piece of her birth mother alive by using her original birth name as her middle name. She couldn't wait to see her parents and thank them.

"MaryAnne continued to live with her Aunt Clara, completed her GED, and found work in her substitute hometown. She continued to be depressed and angry about the birthing experience. MaryAnne regretted that the hospital did not allow her to hold the babies after their delivery. The nurses whisked the babies from the delivery room and out of her life forever. She cried for days knowing that she would never know her daughters and they would never know her. She was terrified about her future and what would become of her.

"Bob continued his education, got his undergraduate degree, and went on to get his master and doctorate of education, and was a teaching assistant for the Dean of Education. He dated but never married; no one interested him as MaryAnne had. Ultimately, he became a professor at the University of Iowa and enjoyed writing non-fiction books and having profound intellectual, philosophical discussions with his colleagues.

"Bob and his father were never close, and after the pregnancy and birth, Bob avoided his father whenever possible. He rarely went home for family holiday events unless his mother called and pleaded for him to make an appearance. Another incident between Bob and his father happened when Bob was a junior in college; after that altercation, Bob never saw his father again. When his father died, he contemplated not going to his funeral but knew the community would gossip, and it would devastate his mother. She begged for a polite appearance, which he did.

"In 2004, ten years after high school graduation, Bob returned to Marshalltown for an all alumni class reunion that coincided with the fall homecoming game. MaryAnne's best friend from high school persuaded her to come back for the weekend events. She had stayed in touch with Jessica Sanders for the last ten years; Jessica kept her up-to-date on the town's news and her old friends. MaryAnne did not plan to attend the banquets and reunion events, but she agreed to go to the homecoming football game with Jessica. There, just a few rows away, sat Bob. His eyes showed surprise yet pleasure at seeing her. He immediately got up and signaled her to meet him at the concession stand. They instantly reconnected. Things progressed from there, and they began a long-distance relationship. He was living and working in Iowa City, and she was still in Minnesota. They finally married in 2005. When MaryAnne moved to Iowa City, he encouraged her to go to college and get her degree. She majored in Kinesiology and then worked as a physical therapist with the U of I football team.

"Their love sustained them through their ordeal, but they felt a loss, an empty place in their hearts for the daughters they were not allowed to keep. About six years ago, while visiting his mother, Bob ran across a file with annual updates and pictures from your adoptive father. When Bob found the documents, he saw your name was Amanda Emily Springs; your parents lived in Pella, and you were going to law school at the University. When confronted, his mother admitted that your adoptive parents agreed on a couple of stipulations as part of the private adoption. First, there would be no contact initiated by the birth parents directly with Emily or any adoptive family member. They agreed to provide Dr. George Myers with an annual update on your health and pictures until you graduated from high school. Bob and MaryAnne followed your success with great pride but honored the legal agreement not to initiate contact. I know they attempted to find your twin sister but to no avail.

"So," Tom continues, "here's some information from your parents in their last letter of instructions. It explains the challenges you will have to claim your share of the inheritance, and it provides a deadline of December 31, 2021, to accomplish the task. If unsuccessful, the estate will be divided in an alternate method as explained in their will. Here's my business card, and as provided in the last letter of instructions, I'm providing you with two DNA test kits; one from AncestryDNA and one from 23andMe. You'll find when you get your test results that Bob and MaryAnne did their DNA a few years ago, hoping that on your initiative, you and your sister would find them. Hopefully, the DNA test results will help you on your journey. Call if I can be of any help. And periodically, please let me know how you are doing. We can meet again closer to the end-of-year deadline, but call, if and when, you find your twin sister."

Amanda is at a loss for words; she sits there and stares at Tom Graves as he pays the bill. When the waiter leaves, Amanda finds her voice. "Tom, thank you for lunch, and thanks for filling in the missing pieces of my life." As he rises to leave, she does the same.

"You're welcome. Call if you have questions or whenever you have information to share." They shake hands, and Amanda steps into the elevator. She gets off on the second floor and finds the entrance to the skywalk.

Amanda strolls back to her office, closes the door, and reads the letter of instructions from her birth parents. She digests the information and then speaks out loud to herself, "Wow! What a day, just when you think you have your life under control, *whamo*, you get yanked in another direction. Like someone throws a switch, and your life goes down a new track."

Chapter 5

◇◇◇◇◇◇◇

Amanda meets Christopher for their afternoon work session. He asks about her luncheon meeting with the mysterious attorney from Iowa City. "I haven't been able to wrap my head around it; my mind is full of his words, but I still can't make much sense of what's happened." She changes the direction of the conversation with "let's get to work." She professionally goes through the steps to review the accomplishments on their task list. Christopher is impressed with what they have completed in just a few days but is worried about Amanda; she seems to be in a contemplative mood.

"Amanda, you seem quiet and unlike your normal self. Are you okay?" She holds back the tears.

"Christopher, are you free this evening? I'd need to talk with someone, and I'd like it to be you." She invites him to her new apartment at the R&T Lofts, one block west of their office. He agrees to swing by HyVee, their favorite local grocery store, to pick up some take-out food from the deli. "Give me twenty minutes; I'll see you at your place."

When he arrives on his first visit to her abode, he remarks on the minimalistic appearance of her loft. It has nice, clean lines, cement floors, and no clutter, but it still feels warm and cozy despite the no-frills. She offers him a beer, grabs one for herself, and leads him to the kitchen. He prepares the food on the dishes she has placed on the counter. "Welcome to my R&T Loft. You may have heard a developer converted the old Des Moines Register and Tribune newspaper building into these modern apartments. It's my new home, and I love it and the location. I can walk to work, and if the weather's bad, I can take the skywalk."

They sit, he confirms how much he likes her apartment, and then he sensitively asks, "What's wrong?"

She shares the luncheon experience and all the details of her conversation with Tom Graves. "My birth parents, whom I never met, left an inheritance for my twin sister and me. But there are strings attached. I have to find her by the end of this year."

Amanda continues to share her life, the life she knew. "As I told you the first night we met, my parents live in Pella, Iowa. Have you ever been to Pella?"

"No, I haven't. I've heard of it each year on the news with something about a flower festival of some kind. Flowers generally are not at the top of my must-see list."

"Really! You've lived in Iowa for four years, and you've never been to the Pella Tulip Festival? It's a wonderful Dutch tradition on the first weekend of May. Growing up in Pella was a blessing; it's a small college town where everyone knows everyone, and there isn't much teenage trouble. Things relax a little during the Tulip Festival, parents lift curfews, and the teenagers gather in the town square for late-night conversations and perhaps a little necking. The local bakery stays open late so everyone can savor one last almond paste-filled Dutch Letter pastry. Doesn't that sound like a dangerous environment for teenagers?"

"My parents were not wealthy, but they were comfortable; probably upper middle income in a small town. Dad is the local insurance agent, and Mom runs her own catering business, mostly for local weddings, birthdays, and anniversary parties. I spent part of my summers helping Mom by carrying trays of food to the various events. I always worried I would stumble and drop one of her creative trays," she chuckles at the memory.

"They provided a loving home, a sense of responsibility, a demand for continuing education, and an expectation of family togetherness. I always enjoyed the fun family weekends, occasional summer vacations, and the many great times with the family. I have two brothers; Brian is five years older, and Mark is three years younger. As the only female, both of my brothers enjoyed teasing me unmercifully, even today." she smiles.

Showing him the two DNA kits, Christopher encourages her to get the process started, "but per the instruction, you'll have to wait for a half-hour before spitting in the tube. You've been drinking beer; guess they don't want drunk silva." Reading the fine print, he explains that it will take six to eight weeks to get the results. "So relax, focus on work, let's have fun, and when the results come in, I'll be there to help you, assuming you want my help."

Chapter 6

◇◇◇◇◇◇◇

Michael Matheson leaves Costco headquarters in Issaquah, Washington. He heads to his nearby condo at the Estates at Cougar Mountain. He loves the location, nestled into the pine trees with the Cougar and Squak mountains surrounding the three-story buildings and clubhouse. Parking in his reserved carport gives him quick access to the centralized mail location. As he enters the lobby, he notices a new face. He greets his new neighbor, who recently moved into the apartment one floor above him.

"Hi, I'm Michael Matheson; I'm your neighbor on the second floor. Didn't you move into Unit 305 last weekend?"

"Yes, I did. I'm Mary Anderson; nice to meet you." He rides the elevator up with her trying to appear sophisticated yet witty.

Leaving the elevator with a smile, he casually comments, "When you're all settled, I'll have you down for a beer or glass of wine and introduce you to some of your new neighbors. Have a nice weekend."

"Same to you."

He unlocks his apartment, steps inside, and does a double-thumbs up to himself, "Alright, alright, that first introduction went well."

He heads to the kitchen, grabs a beer, and steps out onto the patio. The view of the interior courtyard is always inviting, and the pine trees and mountains visible over the adjacent buildings make for a peaceful setting. It's been a long week. Thank God it's Friday.

Returning to the kitchen island, he turns on his computer, scans his new emails, deletes all the junk mail without opening them. Then he sees the message from Ancestry.com. "Your results are IN."

Two months ago, his brother, Matt, sent DNA kits to his sister and him. Matt has dabbled in genealogy for many years and always has new and exciting stories about the family's ancestors and other characters. He suggested our DNA would help him on his latest project.

Matt had been working on family genealogy since high school. Ten years ago, when he was a sophomore, he was required to build a four-generation family tree and then write a short story for his literature class about one of his ancestors. Matt was not particularly excited about the project until talking with close and distant relatives and started piecing together the history of the Matheson family. In the process and research, he discovered that our third great-grandfather had immigrated to the United States from Norway in 1881 and had settled in Decorah, Iowa. Our great-grandfather was born there in 1923. He was sixteen years old when a royal visit by Crown Prince Olav and Crown Princess Mårtha of Norway excited Decorah residents and the Luther College students. It was a big event for this community of Norweigan immigrants.

Twenty-six years later, our grandfather chaired the planning committee for the 1965 Royal visit by Crown Prince Harold V, now the current King of Norway. That story was the centerpiece for Matt's school project. He got an A on his literature piece, as well as his carefully constructed family tree. *Collecting dead ancestors* has had him hooked ever since.

Michael logs into his Ancestry account and immediately sees the DNA match of his brother, Matt, and his sister, Megan. The header on each says: "Close family member - First Cousin." "DUH!" he says out loud, "we're siblings, and I didn't need a DNA test to tell me that." Behind his name on the report was a number, seventeen hundred and eighty-seven, followed by the letters 'cM.' Behind Matt and Megan's was twenty-six hundred and twenty-five cMs. "What the hell is going on here? Why the difference?"

Michael picks up his cell phone and calls his brother. "Did you get your DNA results today from Ancestry?"

"Just walked in the door. Give me a minute, I'll check."

Michael can hear Matt clicking away on the keyboard; he asks Michael if he will sail with them Sunday. Michael says he's looking forward to it and would like to bring his new neighbor, Mary; if I can talk her into going."

"Sure, sure, the more, the merrier."

"Holy shit! What the hell is going on here?" Matt shouts as he looks at his computer screen.

"Those were my exact words. What does this mean?"

Matt seems hesitant, "Give me a few minutes to pull out my old genealogy notes, and I'll come over to your place."

"Okay, pick up a pizza on your way over. Sausage and pepperoni on my half and none of that vegetarian, gluten-free, or cauliflower crust stuff you usually order."

Matt agrees, "Okay, okay. I'll be there in thirty to forty minutes."

Matt arrives with his family tree, iPad, and a messy folder of family genealogy, all balanced on the top of the pizza box. As always, Matt looks like a mad professor. He also seemed anxious or nervous, which is unusual for him. Michael helps him into the condo by taking the file folders off the top of the pizza box and dropping them on the kitchen island by the computer.

They get settled eating the pizza and drinking the first of what will become many Friday night beers. Michael asks, "So, tell me what does this DNA stuff mean and why are you out of sorts. I heard your expletive over the phone when you opened your Ancestry results. Megan and I did this for fun, to help you. Now you seem—I don't know—nervous."

Matt turns, looking directly into Michael's eyes. Slowly Matt responds as if he's carefully picking each word. "I'm sorry, Michael, I never expected we had skeletons in our closet. Pull your computer over here" Michael grabs his laptop and slides it down to their end of the kitchen island. "Start here," Matt says "there you are, here I am, and there's Megan. Do you see anything unusual?"

Michael responds, "Well, I see that the number behind my name is smaller than the one behind yours and Megan's. Care to enlighten me on the difference?"

"Well, first, the cM stands for centimorgans. It's a unit of genetic measurement used by all DNA testing companies. The more centimorgans you share with someone, the more closely you are related."

"So, you and Megan have more centimorgans than you and I? How is that possible?"

Matt frowns, "The test results say Megan and I are full siblings; we are brother and sister."

"I know what a sibling means," Michael responds with irritation. Ignoring his brother's frustration, Matt continues, "It says you are a half brother to us."

"What the fuck!" shouts Michael. "How could that be?"

"Michael, it means that either Mom or Dad isn't your biological parent. Let's compare the shared matches on Ancestry. When I click here, it tells me who shares similar DNA with us. Look, here's our cousin Mary and her daughter, Elizabeth, and here is our mother's brother, Ted. All three of us share similar amounts of centimorgans with them. So, it is safe to say Mom is our biological mother; yours, mine, and Megan's. I will color-code all these shared matches with a yellow dot. We will then know that those with a yellow dot share DNA from our maternal side. It's clear that Dad is not your biological father." Matt clicks away on the computer as he continues the color-coding.

Michael now feels nervous and irritated, "What! Mom had an affair, never told Dad, and just raised me as one of the family?"

"Yes, that would be my guess. Mom would never have expected that we would learn about her secret. Technology and the availability of consumer-DNA testing have changed everything. There are no more biological secrets."

"Consider me pissed off at you for getting me into the middle of your hobby and ruining my happy life. I remember you teased me because my hair was blond and yours was brown; I was tall, and you were short. You always implied I was adopted or that I was the son of the postman. Now, maybe you were right. I can't believe that Dad isn't my dad."

"Michael, Dad is your dad. He raised you, he loved you, and he helped make you who you are today. An unknown biological father is just a sperm donor, a stranger with whom you have no experiences, no memories, and nothing in common, except genes."

Michael runs his hands through his hair. "Oh, for God's sake, who does it say my father is?"

Matt sighs, "I'll spend more time analyzing your DNA to see if it can lead us to discover his name. But do you want to know? What would you do if you found him?"

Michael exclaims, "Beat the shit out of him."

Matt leaves with his messy files and folders and spends the night in his apartment in front of his computer, looking at the related names, trying to make sense of it all. He leaves his apartment early in the morning, grabs some donuts and coffee, and shows up uninvited at Michael's condo.

"Couldn't sleep. I stayed up most of the night. There's no birth father in your DNA results, but there's more interesting unexpected news. Turn on your computer."

"It's already on. I didn't sleep either," Michael replies.

"Take a look at this. You have a strong DNA match to a Robert Myers and a CharlesM. The centimorgans suggest they are your half-brothers. Here's an AmandaS; she's either a half-niece or a half-aunt on your paternal side."

"Jesus, when does this nightmare end?"

Chapter 7

◇◇◇◇◇◇◇

Amanda steps into Christopher's office. She is as excited as a young girl with a new doll at Christmas. "What are you up to tonight? I just got the message from Ancestry that my DNA results are available. I have to finish a brief today. I don't have time to look at it until tonight. Would you care to see what's hidden in my DNA?"

"I'm in, but I don't know how you can wait until tonight; I'd be at it right now."

"I don't have the time today; I'll save it so we can enjoy the adventure together." Leaving his office, she turns back, "Christopher, you should take a DNA test, then I could learn about you."

"Let's wait and see what happens with you first." He smiles and waves her out of his office.

The day seems to go more slowly than most; lots of telephone calls, interruptions by her assistant, and work to draft briefs. She needs to deliver the documents to her boss before the nine o'clock meeting tomorrow. Amanda looks out her office picture window to see a storm brewing. She is mesmerized by the low-hanging clouds, lightning illuminating the sky, and strong winds. She thinks it's just normal Iowa weather for this time of the year, but it seems to match her mood. Exciting and turbulent.

Her office door opens, and Aaron Sloan-Brown walks in, unexpected and uninvited. Aaron is a tall, slim, reasonably nice-looking colleague in his tight-fitting Italian suit. He carries an air of importance about him that is simultaneously sophisticated and irritating. Walking into her office, he makes himself comfortable in one of her upholstered chairs and smiles at her like a Cheshire cat.

"Amanda, I could use your help."

"What can I do for you?" she asks with a smile.

"I'd like your opinion on my new condo. I just moved into the Plaza; it's my grandfather's place, you know, one of the founding partners of our firm. He will spend the year in the south of France, and I'm staying in his penthouse for the next twelve months. It's a terrific place with a romantic night view of the city. I have gotten tired of the immature college kids and decided a more sophisticated place would improve my image. The condo is a little old-fashioned. I'd like to have a woman's point of view on what to store away versus what helps the successful image I want to project. Can you come over this weekend? I'll make you dinner, pour some fine wine, and then give you a tour of my new digs."

Amanda raises her eyebrows, somewhat shocked. "Are you asking me on a date?"

"Yes, but I really would like your help in reorganizing my grandfather's place." He slumps down in the chair, crosses one leg over his knee, and has another wide tooth-filled smile on his face.

Amanda can't believe he's hitting on her. She carefully chooses her words in response. "Aaron, thank you for the offer, but no. I'm not available this weekend, and," she chuckles, "I'm not an interior designer. If you'd see my minimalistic loft, you'd understand I'm absolutely the wrong person to give you advice. But thank you for thinking of me. You should ask Kathryn; I think she might have the decorating talents you need." She stands, walks to the door, opens it, and turns to face him. "You're moving into a lovely building, and it's convenient to the office. Now, Aaron, I have to ask you to leave; I'm up to my eyeballs in work and need to finish a brief today."

Aaron gets up, brushes by her; as he leaves her office, he turns and locks his eyes on her. "I'll invite you over when I've moved, and I have everything in the penthouse settled. See you around." With that parting shot, he closes her door and leaves her standing bewildered. Amanda returns to her desk, sits back, and sighs deeply.

Finally, the day is over; she packs a briefcase for some late-night reading. She's eagerly looking forward to seeing the Ancestry results.

Christopher, always prompt, is waiting for her in the front lobby of the R&T lofts. She collects her mail, and they take the elevator to the fourth floor. On the short ride, she shares the visit by Aaron Sloan-Brown. He shakes his head.

Tossing everything on the credenza just inside the door, she heads to her computer and turns it on. Christopher proceeds to the kitchen for two glasses of wine, hands one to Amanda before grabbing a chair and joining her in front of the computer screen.

"So, what did you say to Aaron?"

"I just got up, opened the door, and asked him to leave. I think he expects to win me over in the future; he didn't take my rejection." She rolls her eyes.

Christopher laughs, "Guess dealing with a college kid with racing hormones wasn't of interest to you." She slaps him playfully on his arm.

"Okay, now what does your AncestryDNA have to say?"

Amanda clicks on the summary. "Well, I guess you can say I'm almost one hundred percent European. My origins are French, English, German, and a little Scandinavian. My twin sister should have a similar profile."

Amanda clicks on the box labeled *'Amanda Springs DNA Matches.'* Christopher looks at the top two matches: Robert Myers - Parent/Child, father's side; Mary-Anne Blanc Myers - Parent/Child, mother's side. "These are my birth parents. A driver going the wrong way on the Interstate killed them in a car accident in 2019. Tom Graves told me that Blanc was her maiden name."

Amanda pulls out a file; she's been researching at the State Historical Library and found more newspaper stories about the accident. She hands the papers to Christopher, who quickly scans the newspaper articles and then studies one picture. "Wow, Amanda, you look just like your mother, but you have your father's eyes. You come by your beauty naturally; they were a beautiful couple."

Amanda looks at Christopher, appreciating the compliment. "Thanks," she replies quietly.

Amanda clicks on her birth mother's name, and there's her ethnicity. "Well, it's clear that my mother is the French side of the family." Clicking on her birth father's name, "he's the English - German side. It looks like they both have a little Scandinavian," Amanda notes.

Christopher adds, "Must have been the Vikings sailing around the European seaports, raping and pillaging all the neighboring countries. How does it feel to see your birth ancestry starting to come to life?"

"It feels like I'm holding a big beautiful rose, and I've just peeled off the first layer. It's exciting to learn where my heritage originated. Isn't it interesting that the English and the French struggled throughout history, but now I have two ancestors who were madly in love with each other in the twentieth and early twenty-first century? It shows if you wait long enough, things can change."

"Yeah, like waiting five hundred years or six or seven generations." Christopher laughs. "Click on the link to see your dad's shared matches. Wow! Look at all the relatives. Logic would tell me, you and your birth father share DNA with all the people on this list.

"But look at the cMs behind each person. They are decreasing as you go down the list. Amanda, type 'cM' in a search engine and give me the full name for this abbreviation and its definition."

Amanda typed in a search and read from her screen, "It says the abbreviation 'cM' stands for centimorgan, which is a unit used to measure genetic linkage. The test result numbers estimate how you and your DNA matches are related. For a parent-child relationship, the number of centimorgans is about thirty-seven hundred, and as the number decreases, the relationship moves further away. It says a website called DNA Painter will convert centimorgans to the possible genetic family relationship. All DNA testing companies report the total amount of shared DNA using centimorgans."

Amanda looks bewildered. Exploring the shared DNA matches with her birth father, she notices three names. The first is labeled MichaelM with centimorgans equal to a half-uncle, the second CharlesM appears to be similar to MichaelM, and the third one, AdamJ, seems to be a full brother. Surprised, Amanda exclaims, "Christopher, this says. I have three close male matches on my birth father's side. There should be a female with enough strength in centimorgans to equate to a full sister, but there isn't one here." Turning to look at Christopher, "There is no sister. What's going on? Where is my twin?"

"Check on your birth mother's side; perhaps she is listed there," Christopher suggests.

"What! Two half-sisters, or possibly aunts on my mother's side named Brittany and Kayla, and here's Adam again but no full sister. Chris, my twin, is not here, either." Amanda sighs, "After waiting all this time, and she does not even appear in my test results."

"That's not logical; the attorney told me that MaryAnne gave birth to twin girls and that our grandfather separated us in the adoption process. I can't believe my birth parents or Tom Graves would send me looking for someone who doesn't exist. So, where do I go from here? How do I find MichaelM, CharlesM, AdamJ, Brittany, and Kayla? I need another glass of wine!"

Christopher grabs the bottle of wine. "Let's go to the rooftop patio. It's a beautiful place, it's a nice night, and you need a break from all this newfound confusion."

Chapter 8

◇◇◇◇◇◇◇

"Hurry, kids, the school bus is here." She hands them their lunch bags, some money to buy something to drink, kisses them on the top of their heads, and watches as they run down the long farm driveway. "I love you," she yells as they reach the door of the bus, "have fun in school."

She can hardly believe school will be out for the summer next week and the children will be home every day. She has yet to plan any outings or activities to keep them occupied for the summer. She knows that it is time to take them on a family vacation, just like they used to do when Garrett was alive. But she just can't find the emotional strength to organize a summer trip.

Last year when Garrett died, she sent them to Y-camp, thinking the week with other children in supervised activities would help them through the loss of their father. She felt the time alone would help her deal with her grief and loss. Unfortunately, her decision was wrong for all of them. In retrospect, she should have kept the family together.

Melissa, who has always been a happy, cheerful daddy's girl, came home from camp quiet and withdrawn. It took a couple of weeks for her to feel comfortable and safe back at the farm.

Marlene on the neighboring farm was a godsend. She brought her girls over every day to play with Melissa and keep her busy. Melissa was still grieving for her father, but Marlene's girls helped her find her way back to being a little girl with imaginative ways to play and enjoy her life.

Last summer, the little eight-year-old girls had only one task: the daily weeding of our garden and Marlene's. Much to everyone's surprise, they stuck with it all summer, and the Tanner and Anderson farms were among the best-maintained gardens for miles around. The girls didn't particularly like the responsibility of weeding and tending the flowers and vegetables, but Tiffany knew it gave them a purpose to start each day. And it allowed Garrett's dad to interact with his granddaughter. They did all the garden work; he provided all the teasing and compliments to bring a smile to their faces. He took a lot of pictures of the girls in the garden and planned to submit some to the local paper to see if they'd run a story on the best three gardeners in the county. The girls didn't believe he would do it until the newspaper arrived in late August. The girls laughed and jumped around like rabbits in their glee. The memory of that day still brings a smile to her face.

Isaac said, "Camp was okay," but he didn't want to go again when the application came for this summer's camp week for seven and eight-year-old boys. He said he would prefer to stay on the farm and do chores with his grandpa. He's only seven, and he is trying hard to be the man of the house. Garrett would be proud of him.

Both Melissa and Isaac are good students, believe in God, and know that their father is in heaven. I wish I had their conviction. I am still angry with God for taking Garrett away from me. He was only thirty-two, a wonderful husband and father. He had big plans for his family's future and dreams for the farm that the Tanner family had continually owned for over one hundred years. He loved being a farmer, particularly the independence of running his own business. He liked the predictable nature of planting, growing, and harvesting, but he didn't like the constant worry about the weather. The dairy cows and livestock required his daily attention, and he tended them with great care; it gave him a lot of pleasure. He loved to stand on the porch at sunset, leaning against the support beams with his coffee cup in hand. He would survey the land and livestock that he managed and thank God for his blessings. Mostly he took pride in his ability to provide for his family.

Sitting with her cup of coffee on the front porch swing, she remembers how he liked routines, especially getting up every morning to go out to his dad's little yellow house on the back of the property. There each morning, they would have coffee at the old Formica kitchen table and plan their day. They made their list of what needed repairing, what fields needed today's attention, who would go to town for supplies. Each day they had a long list of a myriad of many farm details. By late afternoon they were in the dairy barn for the final milking of the day. Then they would come in for dinner in the big house, and they would share all the day's accomplishments. They were a great team on the farm. Now we have a hired hand, Billy Joe, to help run the farm. Life is not the same.

Garrett died of esophageal cancer a year ago last month. It was a terrible death for him and a painful experience for the whole family. He hated that he was exhausted every day, making driving the tractor an impossible chore. Climbing up into the cab sapped all his energy. But each morning, he would walk out to have coffee in the little yellow house and see what easy chores he could do to lighten the farm load. In the end, he was a trooper and never complained when we had to begin providing him with nutrition through the food portal. He died on a Sunday when the children were in Sunday School. He left peacefully as the hospice nurse was administering his daily bed bath.

Dad, like me, still grieves our loss; he comes in from chores at noon each day to make sure I'm okay; his gesture keeps me from feeling alone. Lunchtime was always my time with Garrett. We'd linger over lunch on less busy days, then leave the dishes on the table going to our bedroom for some passionate sex. We loved taking advantage of the quiet, empty house, but we always turned on the radio, just in case Dad or a neighbor came to the house looking for Garrett, which, of course, rarely happened. Perhaps Dad knew about our lunchtime - couples time - routine. She chuckles to herself with memories dancing in her head.

Marlene was always a good neighbor, but last summer, she became my best friend. She was by my side throughout the ordeal of the funeral planning. She organized all the food for the church fellowship hall and ensured everyone who came to the celebration of Garrett's life left the church with a full belly. Except for me, I couldn't eat a bite.

When she brought the girls over each day, she convinced me that I was the one doing her a favor. I remember her words, "Glad to have the girls out of my house during the days."

Each morning when she'd drop the girls off, she would come into my kitchen with a cheerful voice of good morning and muffins, coffee cake, or donuts in her hands. We'd sit a few minutes, just the two of us, to have coffee and much-needed girlfriend time. She was there on the days when I needed a shoulder to cry on, a person to hug, or someone willing to be a good listener.

Usually, we discussed the local gossip of who was doing what at church, who was dancing with whom at the local barn dance, or who did something scandalous in our small community. She was the one holding my hand and being supportive on the days that I doubted I could handle life without Garrett. She listened and was supportive of my concern and obsession that Melissa and Isaac could have inherited a genetic predisposition for cancer from their father. She calmed me when I irrationally felt overwhelmed by even my simplest of daily chores. I couldn't have thanked her enough for the time she gave my family.

When the garden vegetables were ripe and ready for harvest last fall, I sent Marlene an enormous basket of canned goods as an appreciation of her friendship.

I am alone now and find I have no more tears for grieving. The farm needs my daily attention, and my children need to see an occasional smile on their mother's face. I can't imagine my future yet, but I have to start living again and make some decisions.

Chapter 9

◇◇◇◇◇◇◇

Breakfast Sunday morning at Louie's Wine Dive with Chris is always a great way to start my morning. He's at our usual table with a mimosa waiting for me. I never expected I would feel so totally comfortable with anyone, Amanda thinks to herself. "Can life get any better?"

He hands her a stack of papers. He is delighted with his discovery. "It's an organization that helps adoptees find their birth parents. You'll find it on the internet under Search Angels." He points to the top of the page, "Their marketing tag line is: *It's a non-profit organization here to assist you with your genealogy and DNA test results for those seeking help unraveling the past in search of their biological family roots.* Doesn't that describe what you need; help from a genetic genealogist?"

"This is an organization of volunteers who believe that everyone deserves to know who they are and where their ancestors lived. It's as simple as filling out and submitting an application. There is no cost for the service as long as you're not in a hurry."

Amanda looks longingly at Chris across the table. "Did you spend your weekend trying to find a solution to my challenge? I don't know what to say, but I appreciate your interest in helping me with this family journey."

"Amanda, I'm enjoying my time with you, both at work and during our one-on-one time together. I have to admit I've always felt that because I was privileged and spoiled growing up, I would be a self-centered," he pauses to find a different word, then continues, "adult. But now I find I feel your needs are as important or more important than my own. It is an unexpected feeling. I know I'm falling in love with you, and I have no doubt I want you to continue to be in my life."

"Chris, my heart is beating hard. I'm surprised you can't hear it. I've liked you from the day I first met you at Hell, and I've continued to grow more and more interested in having you in my life. You're my first thought when I wake each morning." She smiles broadly and looks into Chris' eyes which are watery and express a sense of caring.

He reaches across the narrow table, places his hand behind her head, and gently brings her forward for a brief but passionate kiss across the table. He softly says, "I'm sure glad we met.

"I have an idea," suggests Chris. "Let's order our breakfast, enjoy Louie's, then call an Uber and go over to my condo. We can check out more of the information on the Search Angel website and consider completing an application. I want to spend the afternoon with you." Amanda smiles in agreement.

The waitress takes their order, and Chris redirects the conversation. "I think you'll like my little place; it's only a one-room studio condo not nearly as big as your loft. I live in the Summit House condominiums at twenty-eighth and Grand, across the street from the old governor's mansion. My folks bought it when I started school at Drake. They preferred ownership rather than spending money on rent. I'm comfortable there; everyone knows everyone, and it's a friendly building community."

Amanda chuckles, "I sold my car when I moved into downtown; it's not like I'm driving around Des Moines looking at properties. But I'm familiar with the area, as I do Uber to Palmer's Deli on Ingersoll, and I think that must be just down the street from you."

"You're right; it's just out my door and down the hill; Palmer's is my usual place for breakfast and dinner. It's a great neighborhood, including a grocery store within walking distance."

"How do you get to work?"

"I usually jog to work; downtown is only a few blocks away. And then I shower and dress in the men's locker room at Hell. But if the weather is terrible, I call Uber or catch a ride with one of my neighbors who works downtown. It's not a problem. I did the same when I was at Drake; it's about the same distance from the condo.

"How about you? I know you walk to work either on the city sidewalk or the skywalk. But how do you get to Pella to visit your parents?"

"I usually go to Pella with my brother, Mark. We try to coordinate our schedules in advance, and we generally are both flexible. I can always rent a car for a weekend, especially if I want to combine shopping at the mall with a trip to Pella the next day. Avoiding car payments, parking issues, buying gas, and paying insurance premiums work for my budget. An occasional rental is a reasonable solution, plus Mom comes into Des Moines to shop at least once or twice per month, so we get girl time and lunch together. Living downtown is convenient, and like your place, I'm just a few steps away from local farmer's markets, grocery stores, entertainment, and many great restaurants. It's a perfect lifestyle for me. What more could a girl want, other than a handsome guy by her side?" she smiles innocently at Chris.

Chris logs into his Uber app and requests a car. He pays the check and escorts Amanda out of Louie's. They arrive at his condo in just a few minutes. He reaches out with his key fob unlocking the interior security door. "I call this my lock-and-leave condo. The security system requires this electronic key to gain access, and the video cameras record the activities at the doors."

Up the elevator to the second floor, Chris unlocks

the door to his unit. He leads the way, shuts the door, turns, and gently presses her body against the wall. His eyes stare at her lips hungrily. Chris gently leans in and brushes his lips against Amanda's. He pulls back and looks at her, waiting for her reaction. Slowly, a smile breaks out. It seems like the feelings are mutual. He presses closer and enjoys exploring. Her mouth, breath, and scents all stimulate his senses. He finds it difficult to pull away from her but finally grabs her hand and brings her into his living area.

Chris starts to walk over to the computer to pull up the Search Angel information. His hands are on the keyboard, but before entirely typing the first word, he feels Amanda's hand pull at his.

He looks at her and sees the desire in her warm brown eyes. She slowly leads him over to the bed. She sits on the edge of the mattress and looks up at Chris. Slowly, she starts unbuckling his pants. He is so hard that his bulge is straining against his zipper. She unzips his pants, and as she does, Chris remembers that he did not get to his laundry the night before and is not wearing any briefs. She looks up at him and sees the pleasure on his face. He moans as her tongue moves slowly across her lips; he feels as though he may explode. She starts kissing his stomach and starts moving downward. Before she can go any farther, he kicks his jeans off and presses her against the bed. He pulls his shirt over his head, not caring that he hears a button roll across the floor. Amanda is lying on the bed, watching him. Chris slowly starts to unbutton her shirt, savoring each moment. Her skin is lightly tanned and soft. As he pulls her shirt away, he sees the sexy, lacy bra, and he catches his breath. Impatient, Amanda sits up and takes it off. Chris is in awe of her perfectly shaped breasts. He impatiently unbuttons her jeans and pulls them off. Apparently, she forgot to do her laundry, too. He sits back and memorizes every curve of her body. He leans over and gently kisses her. Amanda pulls his body down on hers, craving the feel of his body against hers. His hand reaches down to caress her and feels the wetness between her legs. Chris cannot hold back any longer. Slowly, he guides himself into the warmth, releasing a breath he did not realize he was holding. Amanda takes in his width and wraps her legs around his waist, taking him in deeper. She starts to rock her hips as Chris grabs her waist and thrusts faster and faster. They looked into each other's eyes; the release was coming too soon. Amanda leans her head back and cries out as her orgasm overtakes her. When he hears her cries, he lets go and finds his release. Spent, Chris collapses on Amanda's body. He pulls back his head and sees the satisfied look on her face. They both smile knowingly. Their relationship would never be the same again.

"*Wow*! Could I order another Sunday just like this one? This day has been amazing." Amanda stretches her body like a purring cat, signaling that she too enjoyed their time together.

He realizes that they haven't eaten since breakfast. Chris finds the menu for Centro, one of his favorite downtown restaurants, and places an order for dinner. While they wait for the delivery, Amanda uses the bathroom to freshen up and redress. She finally takes in his condo. He's right; it is tiny; but perfect for a single man. It's a bachelor's pad in a charming area of town. All his needs for sleeping, eating, and showering are within five hundred and fifty square feet. The bed here, TV and chairs in the center, and kitchenette and eating area. What more could a guy need?

Chris grabs a chilled bottle of wine, two wine glasses, and they go out on the balcony to enjoy the air. It's a beautiful Iowa night, with warm temperatures, unusually low humidity, and a great view over the softly lit swimming pool. The food arrives, and they stay on the balcony enjoying the evening. Chris reaches for her hand, turns it, and gently kisses her palm. "I can't tell you how wonderful this day has been for me." She stares into his eyes and assures him it has been a wonderful day for her as well.

It's almost nine o'clock and tomorrow is a workday. Chris reluctantly orders an Uber to take her back to her loft. They walk together to the entry door on the first floor. While they wait, he turns and wraps her in his arms and presses his lips to hers. "Love you," he says, and she responds the same.

The Uber arrives too quickly, and the magical day is over. It's back to reality; tomorrow is another day at Hell.

Chapter 10

⋄⋄⋄⋄⋄⋄⋄

The telephone rings and Amanda eagerly lunges for her cellphone, thinking it must be Chris. "Hi, good looking."

"Good evening. Is this Amanda Springs?" a stranger asks.

Somewhat embarrassed, Amanda replies, "I'm sorry, I was expecting someone else. Yes, this is Amanda. May I ask who is calling?"

"Amanda, you don't know me; my name is Jennifer. I'm a genetic genealogist with Search Angels. You completed an application asking for a volunteer to help you find your birth father, birth mother, and sibling. I'm that volunteer."

"Thank you for calling, Jennifer. I'm excited to hear from you and to have your help."

"Is now a good time." Jennifer inquires.

"Oh, yes, yes, of course," Amanda replies anxiously, wanting answers to her questions.

"I've sent you an email that outlines the process, what you can expect, and the instructions on providing your DNA results to me. Amanda, most requests are for the free basic search that we do at no cost. But sometimes, people need to learn about their family ancestors more quickly. In those situations, the adoptee pays for services that guarantee a steady amount of work by the volunteer each week. So, let's start there. You seem to have some urgency; why did you pay to have someone researching steadily to find your birth parents?"

"A couple of things, part of it is just my personality; I like to solve problems, and I'm prone to take action to get it done. But the real reason is I have a deadline; I have to find my twin sister by December 31."

Jennifer refrains from asking "why?" knowing that the reason will be forthcoming. "According to the application, you are searching for your birth mother, birth father, and a sibling."

"I now know the names of my birth parents."

There's a long pause before Jennifer proceeds, "Amanda, I'm a little confused. If you know the names of your birth parents, why did you submit an application asking for help to find them?"

"Yes, it's complicated. I know my birthparent's names because my DNA results identified them specifically, and a few weeks ago, an attorney told me about them and their story. But I still want you to verify that I'm reading these DNA results correctly.

"I've learned that a drunk driver tragically killed my birth parents in a car accident, and I've researched the facts through the newspapers. Bottom line, I am named in their will, but to participate in the distribution of their estate, I have to find my twin sister. In my DNA test results, Jennifer, you will see that Ancestry lists my birth parents' names as Robert Myers and MaryAnne Blanc Myers. The attorney said they had submitted their DNA four years ago, hoping my sister and I would find them, but they died before that happened."

"Are you saying that you are now only looking for your twin sister, an unknown sibling?" she inquires.

"Well, she's my most important goal, but the DNA has raised additional questions. It appears to my novice analysis that I also have three close male relatives on my birth father's side and two close females on my mother's side. Until now, I didn't have any idea these relatives existed."

"Amanda, what about your twin sister? Do you see a female with about twenty-six hundred centimorgans of a shared match?" she inquires. "No, not in the results from Ancestry. Can you find her without a DNA match?"

"No, I can't," Jennifer states with a firm conviction. "DNA doesn't work that way. I'm sorry to tell you that she will be lost unless your twin sister is looking for you and takes a DNA test. I can do some research to determine more about your birth parents, your grandparents and try to determine the relationship behind your other five close relatives, but your twin sister is not going to be in this mix."

"Yes, I need your help and appreciate your time in figuring out all these relationships."

"Tell me what research you've already done to find your twin sister."

"I've been to St. Cloud, Minnesota, our birthplace, and talked with the Clerk of Courts, who confirmed that twins were born on that date. St. Cloud Social Services, however, has no record of anyone adopted with my birth date. I checked the internet on documents available from the State, but no information is available."

"OK, you've taken all the obvious initial steps. Tell me what you know about your birth parents."

"I know little." Amanda shared the details given to her by Tom Graves and information from the newspaper articles.

"That's quite a bit; most adoptees have little to no information. Often all their adoptive families have told them is that they were adopted. OK, Amanda, I think we are ready to get started. You have my email address from the message I sent you, and you have my cell phone number from your caller-ID. Contact me anytime you have new information or have a question. I have your contact information from the application form. Do you have any questions before we start working on your DNA journey?"

"Nothing that I can think of right now."

"Amanda, before we hang up, one last thing. There will be times when we need to contact close relatives to find what they know about a birth in the family. I will call you or send an email before I contact anyone with more than three hundred centimorgans of a shared match to you; I will need your permission to proceed with the call. If it's a closer relationship, I will need you to make the call. Does that work for you?"

"Yes, Jennifer, contact me when and if that scenario comes up. We can discuss it then," Amanda acknowledges.

"Great. It's no big deal, but I want to ensure that you control when I contact your closely related birth family members. I'll wait for your email granting me access to your DNA and get back to you within four or five days. I'm anxious to get my first look at your matches."

"Jennifer. I look forward to this adventure, even though I understand it will not help me find my twin sister. Maybe one of these five newly found relatives knows something that will help find her. Thanks for calling, and thanks for all you do as a volunteer."

Amanda grabs her cell phone and sends a text message to Christopher. "Search Angel just called; want to hear details?" She adds multiple question marks and multiple emoji hearts. "Your place or mine; say six tomorrow evening?" She adds another smiling emoji and hits send.

Amanda logs into the internet and reads Jennifer's email. She sends a message to Jennifer giving her access to her AncestryDNA test results and explains that she doesn't have her 23andMe test results yet.

Chapter 11

◇◇◇◇◇◇◇

Wanting to get an early start, Amanda walks to the bank of elevators for a quick ride on the high-speed elevator to the twenty-second floor. The senior partners are one floor up and accessible by a wide sweeping staircase between the two levels. Clients arrive on the twenty-third floor to the impressive reception area, which is well-appointed and makes a clear statement about the firm's success. The twenty-second floor is where all the detailed work gets done.

As she reaches to press the elevator button, a hand suddenly appears on the button, and an arm wraps around her waist. "Good morning, good lookin' you're starting early, as usual." She turns with a smile and finds she is just inches away from his lips. The elevator door closes, and they are alone for a quick ride to their floor. He leans her against the elevator wall and kisses her softly at first, and then allows the kiss to develop into something more passionate. She's immediately aroused and knows her desire shows in her red cheeks and the passion in her eyes. She sees the feelings are mutual. As the elevator begins to slow, he pulls away reluctantly. Standing close, he whispers in her ear, "I have a question. Are you wearing under that dress what you were wearing under your jeans last night?"

The elevator door opens. Christopher quickly steps out, looks back over his shoulder with a broad smile, "Have a great day, Ms. Springs." She's momentarily stunned and stands in the elevator without moving; she finally reaches out her arm to prevent the door from closing. As she steps out of the elevator, she sees Christopher walking briskly toward his office, and she hears him chuckling.

As she reaches her office, she checks her calendar. The day has started with pleasurable sensual feelings, but since they are working closely for the next several hours, it will be challenging to keep her mind on business. They have an interview at ten o'clock with their client, Darla Wilson, followed by a meeting to debrief what they learn, and finally, they will work together to draft questions for the deposition of Lark Monahan. At the end of the workday, they plan to spend more time in her loft. She smiles as she imagines how this day will end.

She reviews the interview questions and makes a mental note of the ones she will ask and those Christopher will pursue. She wants these questions to appear spontaneous and not staged. To get to the truth, Darla needs to feel comfortable. Sharing her perspective about the events that led to the charge of embezzlement is an essential part of the discovery. Amanda checks with her assistant, Lisa, and confirms that the court reporter has already arrived and has set up her stenotype machine in an inconspicuous corner of the conference room. All appears to be ready for the morning.

Darla arrives promptly at ten o'clock; the receptionist escorts her down the impressive staircase to the front conference room. She appears unhappy and presents a definite aura of defensiveness. All one hundred and fifty pounds on her five-foot four-inch body display that she means business and is offended by all that is transpiring. She carries an unbecoming frown on her face, worried wrinkles on her forehead, and a no-nonsense demeanor that shouts, 'I'm in charge here.' Her quick gait amplifies her determination with each advancing step. Amanda sighs and thinks to herself that making Darla comfortable will be a challenge.

Christopher makes his presence known beside Amanda with the brush of his arm against hers. He watched the same parade down the steps into the conference room. He turns his head, smiles, and remarks, "Well, I think our client just arrived; let's go see what she has to say."

The meeting lasted more than two hours. It was a fascinating meeting with an angry, upset client. We now have her side of the facts and can provide an update and some insight for Davis III. The court reporter quickly packs up her equipment and agrees to have the transcript available by noon tomorrow. Thanking her for her work, Christopher helps her carry out her equipment; while Amanda readies the lunch her assistant has brought in.

Christopher returns, and they settle back into their chairs for a working lunch hour. Laptop open and ready, she turns and smiles, "That was quite an experience; have you ever seen anyone that animated and angry. What did you make of it?"

"Do you want the facts I heard, my perceptions of her behavior, or the laws affecting this case," he replies.

"Let's start with the client's facts."

"OK, our client stated that Lark Monahan hired her because she was an experienced bookkeeper. His business had grown quite large, and he needed help on the financial side. He needed a bookkeeper to manage the accounts receivable and accounts payable. Additionally, Lark liked her prior 'watchdog' experience in finding and eliminating unnecessary business expenses including inappropriate charges by employees on their reimbursement vouchers."

Amanda interjects, "And he agreed to give her fifty percent of any money she saved him. She stated he didn't include it as part of her salary but wrote a check she described as *under the table.* Darla processed it as a business expense at his direction. But she was clear that what he did was illegal; it should have been on her paycheck, and he should have submitted state and federal withholding taxes.

"She claims no issues or complaints with any former employers for whom she did the bookkeeping. We will need to call them to see if we can verify her claim. She received regular annual performance appraisals from Mr. Monahan, and she freely admits he talked with her about the late payment of vendor invoices on her last review. She has copies of her appraisals and will make them available to us.

"After a year as his bookkeeper. she saved him a great deal of money; she doesn't know how much, but he paid her regularly under the table for her fifty percent of the savings. After the first year, he asked her to take over payment of his non-business bills to relieve him of that burdensome task."

Amanda suddenly feels his foot slowly moving up and down her leg under the table. "Christopher, please," she lets out a slow, longing breath, "I can't focus when you do that."

He quickly swivels her chair toward him, reaches for her, and gives her a slow kiss. "Don't you think you could call me Chris? All my friends do, and I consider you more than a friend."

"OK," she pauses, "I would love to call you, Chris. You will have my full attention at the loft tonight," she promises with a smile. "But right now, we need to continue debriefing our interview and preparing for our meeting with Davis III tomorrow."

"OK, just one more thing, you didn't answer the question I asked on the elevator this morning." She feels herself getting warm and is sure her cheeks are bright red. "Oh God, Amanda, can't I just check now and relieve the suspense."

Slapping him on the arm, she hands him his pen. "Work!"

Chris gives her a lopsided grin and reluctantly returns to work. "Darla claims she was surprised when the CPA came into her office and told her they were performing a non-scheduled but routine audit of the books. The CPA instructed her to go home. She claims she left the car dealership without any concerns. Mr. Monahan called her back to the dealership on Friday and allowed her the opportunity to resign or be fired. She resigned, knowing the trust they'd built over two years was gone. Subsequently, on the advice of his CPA, Lark Monahan filed a police report for the embezzlement of nearly $97,000. The Polk County Attorney's office took over from there, filing the felony charges against Darla."

Amanda adds, "She further claims Monahan knew he shouldn't have been paying her under the table and feared she would report him. So, according to her, he threw her under the bus and charged her with embezzlement.

"Chris, are we in agreement that these are the facts as related by Darla? Do we need to make any changes?"

"Let's read the transcript tomorrow before we meet with Davis III and see if there's anything we've missed. But I think we've nailed it. What do you think; are you ready to quit for the day and retire to your loft?"

"Chris, you have a one-track mind; and I'm on that same track," she says, smiling mischievously. We can discuss our perceptions over dinner and in the morning document Iowa's law regarding first-degree theft."

As they unlocked the door to Amanda's loft, the sexual tension was palpable. As the door closes, he turns her toward him, takes a shallow breath. "I've been waiting for this moment all day." With a gleam in his eye, he pulls her toward him and gives her a long, lingering kiss.

"OK, now will you finally tell me if you are wearing panties or going commando." She suggests he check it out for himself. Wrapping her warmly in his arm, he runs his hand slowly under the hem of her dress and up her smooth leg. Suddenly he stops, excited to discover that his fingers are against a hot moist sensitive spot. He can't help but roll his fingers slowly, feeling the growing pleasure it creates for them both. She moans with pleasure. Without a moment's hesitation, he guides her to the bed. He can't wait another minute.

Chapter 12

◇◇◇◇◇◇◇

Michael reaches for his ringing cell phone. "Hello, Matt."

"Michael, I have been consumed building your family tree based on the DNA matches from Ancestry. Want to hear what I've found?" asks his brother.

"No, I think I'll pass," he pauses and then shouts with exasperation, "of course, I want to hear. Get your ass over here; I'll have a cold beer ready."

"Better make it two. I'll be right over."

Matt arrived within fifteen minutes. As usual, he looks as though he has slept in his clothes. Loaded down with files, his iPad, and stacks of paper make him look considerably disorganized. He drops everything on the kitchen counter.

Popping open a can of beer, Michael hands it to

his brother. "Am I going to like what you are about to show me?"

Matt chuckles, "There is nothing here to like or dislike. It's only a roadmap to your genetic family.

"It was much easier than I thought to trace your paternal family line. When we first looked at the DNA results, we were shocked by our half-sibling relationship that the significance of other DNA matches didn't register with me. Your birth father is not listed," he pauses, then smiles, "but his biological son, Robert Myers, is." He points and taps his finger at the screen. "Your match to him was there waiting to be interpreted. Let me show you."

Matt clicks on DNA matches and scrolls down to the three siblings. "Here's what we were looking at yesterday. Now, if I scroll up to the top, here's your half-brother on the paternal side. And here are three other close relatives, CharlesM, AdamJ, and AmandaS. Per the centimorgans, Charles is Robert's brother, Adam is Robert's son, and Amanda is Robert's daughter.

"We get half our DNA from our biological mother, and the other half from our biological father, and our parents got half from each of their parents.

"You said when you found your birth father, you would 'beat the shit out of him.' I'm sorry to say you won't get that chance. I found your brother, Robert Myers, on the internet. A drunk driver killed him and his wife in a head-on collision in 2019. Here's the newspaper account of the accident." He hands the story to Michael and sits quietly as his brother reads the newspaper article:

Deaths on Interstate 80

By Ronald Stelzer

IOWA CITY — A vehicle traveling west in the eastbound lane of Interstate 80 near Iowa City last evening fatally collided with another car. All three persons involved in the accident were taken to the University of Iowa Hospital. The driver of the wrong-way vehicle had non-life-threatening injuries was examined and then taken to the Johnson County Jail on suspicion of criminal vehicular operation. The man and woman in the other vehicle were dead on arrival at the hospital.

"I also found their obituary in the *Iowa City Press-Citizen* that included a picture of Professor Myers and his wife." Matt hands him the article, "it says that Professor Myers' father is deceased."

Iowa City Couple Killed on I-80

By Ronald Stelzer

IOWA CITY — University of Iowa Professor Dr. Robert K Myers (45) and his wife of fifteen years, MaryAnne (Blanc) Myers (44), were killed in a head-on collision on Interstate 80 Thursday.

Dr. Myers was the son of the late George and Toni (Floden) Myers, Marshalltown, Iowa. MaryAnne was the daughter of Jon and Gabriella Blanc, Dallas, Texas.

After high school, Dr. Myers attended the University, completing his undergraduate degree, a master's and doctorate in education. He has worked at the university since 2004 and was promoted to a full professor in 2010. He will be missed by the many graduate-level education students who took classes from him. His wife, MaryAnne, worked for the University Athletic Department as a physical therapist.

Survivors include two daughters, Brittainy (David) Evans, Appleton, Wisconsin; Kayla Sheets, Tracy,

California, and one son, Adam Jacob Myers, Iowa City.

Services will be held at Zion Lutheran Church tomorrow at 11:30 a.m. Interment will be at the North Hill Memorial Cemetery in Marshalltown, where a private family graveside service will be held. Larson Funeral & Cremation Services, Iowa City, is in charge of the arrangements.

"Look at this picture, Matt. I could be looking in a mirror. We have the same nose structure, a left ear that sticks out a little, dimples, full lips, and a receding hairline. Wow! No doubt we carry similar genes.

"I don't get it. If Robert Myers is my half-brother, he doesn't appear to have a surviving brother named Charles; or at least he's not named in the obituary. He has a son, Adam. Neither daughter in the obit is named Amanda. Please tell me you know why."

"Sorry, Michael, I don't know. The DNA clearly shows Amanda is their child. The obituary confirms that Adam Myers is your half-nephew, and he is living in Iowa City.

"How about sending a message to Charles on Ancestry; acknowledge that you are a closely related relative per your DNA results. You don't have to tell him that you are his half-brother in your first communications. Let's draft a message and see if he responds."

Michael and Matt work together to craft a message. They click on the send key, jettisoning the message through the magic of the internet. There is nothing to do now but wait for a response.

"Matt, what about Amanda. The obituary did not list her as a daughter of Robert Myers."

"Here's my guess: there is a Kayla Sheets; perhaps her full name is Amanda Kayla Sheets. People generally try to disguise their names on Ancestry to protect their identity."

"How did Mom meet and have sex with George Myers?"

Matt replies, "No clue, but DNA does not lie. Maybe she shared some information with Megan; you know, mother and daughter confidential conversation."

"Matt, we are not going to discuss Mom's sex life with Megan; promise me that you will keep this all confidential."

"No worries. Megan knows that you are a half-brother; she's seen her DNA results and figured it out."

"Well, if she asks, my official answer is 'I don't believe it,' and I'll take another test to prove it's an error."

Just then, they heard a ping sound on Michael's iPad; a message had arrived from Ancestry. They both thought Charles had already responded to their message. Matt looks with surprise at his brother, "He must have been sitting at his computer."

Michael opens the message and reads it out loud to

Matt. "Hi, my name is Amanda; I am working with a genetic genealogist to unravel the mystery of my AncestryDNA matches. You are closely related to me. I was adopted at birth and am looking for my biological family. My genealogist would like to know the names of your paternal grandparents. Would you be willing to share your information? I would appreciate your help."

"How do I respond? How much do I tell her?" Matt looks to his brother for advice.

"I don't think there are any rules here. Tell Amanda as much as you'd like."

Michael begins typing a return message. "Amanda, like you, I am looking for my birth father. My birth mother raised me, and I had a wonderful Dad, who I've recently learned is not my biological father. I can't tell you how strange all of this is for me. My brother is our family genealogist, and he's determined through his research that my birth father was George Myers. Per a newspaper article in the *Iowa City Press-Citizen*, Dr. Robert Myers, his son, was killed in a car accident in 2019. I just learned these facts today. What can you tell me about the Myers family and our DNA connection?" He quickly clicked the send button before he could change his mind.

They waited, but there was no reply.

Chapter 13

⬦⬦⬦⬦⬦

A first for her. She let a man spend the night. They were both satisfied and comfortable. It was too much effort to insist that he crawl out of her cozy bed and go home. He had snuggled, kissed, and tickled her until she finally agreed he could spend the night.

Amanda rolls on her side to kiss Chris, only to realize that he isn't in bed. She sits up, and across the loft, she sees him busy in her kitchen making breakfast—what a treat. She grabs her bathrobe, scurries across the cold floor, finds a seat at the counter, and greets him. "Good morning."

Chris hands her a cup of coffee with a smile on his face, "I can't believe how great you look in the morning; no make-up, messy hair, and you look stunning."

Amanda returns his smile, "You can stay over anytime if you're going to make my breakfast and deliver coffee with compliments like that."

As he prepares breakfast, Amanda brings him up-to-date on her DNA search. "Chris, I meant to tell you last night, but I was more interested in my time with you under the covers." She smiles coyly at him. "I had a conversation with Jennifer. I've sent her my login information, and she's already working to discover who all these relatives are, and she will tell me more about my birth parents and their parents. There's one problem, my 23andMe results arrived yesterday. There's no twin sister. I am not going to find my twin sister unless she submits her DNA. What are the odds that will happen before the end of the year when it hasn't happened in the last decade?"

"Sounds like an impossibility. So what happens to your share of the estate if you don't find your twin sister?"

"I don't know. I didn't ask that question. If I don't find my twin by November, I'll ask Tom Graves that question."

Over breakfast, the conversation shifts to business. They are meeting with Davis III at three o'clock to update him on the meeting with Darla Wilson. Their goal is to share their findings on Iowa law regarding first-degree theft, then provide him a list of questions for the deposition of Lark Monahan.

"The transcript from the court reporter will arrive by noon," Amanda reminds Chris. "Let's each take an hour to review the transcript, then meet at one o'clock to make any changes to our interview notes. Your office or mine, Chris?"

"Come to my office. Based on what we heard from Darla, I've drafted some questions for the Monahan deposition. I'll email you a copy, and you can review and add any questions before we meet at one."

Grabbing her cell phone, "Here's an airdrop to your cell phone. I drafted some notes on the Iowa theft laws; they are reasonably straightforward and clear. A criminal charge of theft generally requires the specific intent to permanently deprive another individual of their property. I think the prosecutor can quickly get to her intent; she will not return the money because she believes she earned it.

"As for Lark Monahan, once he had evidence that Darla embezzled his money, he wanted her held responsible. The law requires a complaint along with the evidence to be filed with the police department. And that's what he did.

"As for penalties, like many states, Iowa classifies its theft offenses according to the value of the stolen property. The law states that thefts involving property or services valued at greater than ten thousand dollars are first-degree thefts, the highest theft offense level. If convicted, Darla could face a maximum ten-year prison sentence and a fine of up to ten thousand dollars. I don't think powerful politician Daddy is going to want to see his daughter sent to prison.

"Do we have a date yet for the court's pretrial conference? I am eager for the exchange of the witness lists and the prosecutor's discovery documents."

Chris replies that he doesn't recall the date, but he'll check in the office and take it as part of the review with Davis III.

"Wonderful breakfast Chris. I'll clean up the kitchen while you head home to shower and dress. Unless, of course, you want to shower here and wear the same suit you wore yesterday; you know the one you removed quickly and threw on the floor last night."

"Very funny, Miss Springs; I'll see you in the office within the hour." He texts an Uber and waltzes her to the door with a slow, lingering kiss. Just as the door is about to close, he pushes it back open, "Did I tell you I had a wonderful time last night, and I love you?"

She smiles and leans in for another quick kiss. "See you soon." Closing the door, she leans back against it with a smile on her face and sighs, "I could get used to having him around."

She quickly cleans the kitchen, turns on the TV for the local news, and dashes down the hall to the shower. She smiles as she passes by the bed and sees last night's dress left in a ball on the floor; she picks it up and adds it to her dry-cleaning bag. Guess we were both in a hurry, she smiles to herself. Forty minutes later, she's ready for work and dressed appropriately for her meeting with Davis III.

As she opens the door to leave, she hears a ping on her computer. She changes direction and goes back to her desk. It's a message from Jennifer. "I found your birth father's brother, Charles Myers. His last known address appears to be in Marshalltown, Iowa. Robert and Charles were both born in Marshalltown, as were your paternal birth grandparents. Could you make contact with Charles through Ancestry messaging and see if he would correspond with you? Your goal is to hear about your birth parents, your grandparents, and anything he might know about Michael, your half-uncle, and your brother, Adam." She quickly replies and agrees to make contact. She makes a note to herself to deal with it this evening and dashes out the door for work.

As she arrives at her office building, Amanda sees Kathryn Baker waiting for the elevator. Amanda recalls that Kathryn had shared she was born in Ireland and adopted by an American family. Being an adoptee herself, Amanda feels terrible that she hadn't taken the time to have lunch with her to discuss their commonality. "Good morning, Kathryn; how are things going for you in the tax department?"

"I couldn't be happier. My boss is great; he's given me some interesting and meaningful work. I feel challenged every day. How about you? How's the embezzlement case?"

"It's moving along nicely, still a lot of work to be done before we go to court. Rather, I should say before Davis III goes to court. Are you doing anything special for lunch today?"

Kathryn holds up a brown paper bag. "I'm planning to have lunch at my desk."

"'Want company? I can grab a sandwich at the deli. Come to my office, Kathryn; I found a small, private conference room I want to show you. What time do you normally eat lunch?"

"Anytime works. Would twelve-thirty be ok?"

The elevator door opens, and as they step out, Amanda confirms the time, and Kathryn agrees, "I'll come down to your office. See you then. Have a good morning."

And it was a good morning. Amanda met with two potential clients; two young women who belong to her Rotary Club are starting a fantastic new business and need help with filing for incorporation and a myriad of other start-up issues. They are looking for a long-term relationship with an attorney who can assist them in developing a workable contract. Amanda was excited to learn about their business strategy and ideas. They are interviewing three different lawyers before selecting the one they feel will be the most compatible with them. She was at her best this morning in marketing her legal skills and what she could bring to the table. She liked their ideas and found them to be wise, savvy businesswomen. She escorts them to the elevator and expresses her desire to do their legal work. Returning to her office, she makes a note to follow up with a hand-written note to thank them for their consideration.

Amanda left the office to grab a sandwich for lunch. She returned just in time. Kathryn was waiting at her office door. She raises her hand above her head and beckons Katheryn to follow her. "Let's go around the corner to the conference room; we can eat there."

The room is at the end of the hall by the back staircase; just one six-foot rectangular table, a credenza along the back wall, and two straight back upholstered chairs. "Amanda, I like this room. It's a perfect place to work on complicated cases." They unpack their lunch and make themselves comfortable.

"Kathryn, when we had drinks after work on our first day, you stated that you were born in Ireland and adopted by American parents. You were sharing a personal story, but there wasn't any conversation or dialogue about it that night. I want you to know, adoptive parents raised me, but my birth was not in an exotic location or a foreign country. Unless you consider St. Cloud, Minnesota exotic," she chuckles. Amanda explains the circumstances of her birth and the search she has underway to find her twin sister. She tells her about Jennifer, her search angel, and the recent discovery of four other close relatives. Amanda continues, "I've known since I was a little girl that my parents were not my biological parents. How about you?"

"My adoptive parents were extremely wealthy. As a baby, they raised me by hiring a series of nannies. My parents loved to show me off to their friends and demonstrate that we were a loving, cohesive family. It wasn't the truth; it was a facade. They raised me in luxury and comfort, but as I grew up, I became their servant. I cleaned the house, made beds, and learned to cook their meals from the age of eight. I couldn't wait to graduate from high school and go on to college. I threw myself into my education in mathematics and finance. I then decided to go on to law school. My father died of a heart attack three years ago, and Mom has been traveling the world ever since; I haven't seen her in the last eighteen months."

"I'm so sorry, Kathryn. It's such a contrast to my fun, carefree childhood. Have you ever wanted to find your birth parents?"

"Yes, I found my birth mother last year. She left a note at the adoption agency saying she would love to meet me if I wanted to reach out to her. We have a nice relationship; it's more like friends instead of a mother-daughter relationship. We meet each other monthly to have lunch or dinner, and we've even shared some holiday time and travel experiences."

"What about your birth father?"

"Not interested. I haven't done a DNA test and never will. I don't want him or any of his descendants to find me."

"Why do you feel that way? I don't want to pry, but I'm a friendly listener."

"I don't mind sharing with you; I've had enough psychological counseling in my life that I'm now comfortable in my skin. My birth mother came from a Catholic family; her boyfriend's father raped her just before her sixteenth birthday. Her parents didn't believe her, assumed she was lying, and then accused her of provoking the situation. They sent her to the home for unwed mothers in Ireland. They didn't want her situation to embarrass the family; they sent her away. My birth mother has shared how depressed and lonely she was in Ireland. Two weeks after giving birth, she was put on a plane and returned to her parents. No warmth, no caring; it was like a business transaction. The nurses took the baby from the delivery room to the new parents; they agreed I was physically acceptable. Two days later, my adoptive parents joyfully took me from the hospital to start a new life. My birth mother received no information from the hospital, and we had no way to find each other in the future."

Amanda reaches across the table, takes her hand, and gives it a warm tight squeeze. "Each adoptee has a different experience; often, an adoptee has a better life than would have been experienced had they been raised by their birth parents. Adoptive parents are generally screened, better educated, and in a better financial position. That is not always the situation; I'm glad you found your birth mother and have a warm relationship with her."

"Amanda, one question; it has nothing to do with adoption. How do I reserve this room if I want to use it?"

"It's not difficult. Open that drawer in the credenza." She points to the left drawer. "Write your name on the calendar for the dates and times you want, and it's yours."

She watches as Kathryn writes her name to reserve the room for tomorrow afternoon. She looks up and smiles at Amanda; "I'll be your neighbor tomorrow;

I do have a complicated case that I'd like to review without interruptions."

"Amanda, thanks for sharing lunch with me. I feel I have found someone who understands how it feels to be adopted. I appreciate the heads up on this room. I'll have to let my boss know where he can find me; I could be here often." They clean up the room and leave it as they found it.

"Have a great afternoon."

Amanda returns to her office and finds Chris waiting for her. "Did you forget our meeting?" Chris asks.

"What meeting?" checking her calendar, which has nothing on it for the afternoon. She looks up with confusion on her face.

"I'm just kidding. I missed you when I couldn't find you for lunch."

She grabs a piece of paper, crunches it into a ball, and sends it his way as a missile.

"Leave, Mr. Reed; I have billable hours to create."

She smiles as he gets up from the chair and salutes her as he walks out the door. "Yes, ma'am. See you tonight."

Chapter 14

◇◇◇◇◇◇◇

After a busy morning reviewing Chris' deposition questions, she had an additional one. She sent a reply to Chris and then spent the balance of the morning on other calls and billable work for other clients. By noon the transcript arrived, and she carefully read through the dialogue from yesterday's meeting with Darla Wilson. Amanda was satisfied their brief for Davis III was complete.

She sent everything to the printer, making two copies; and saving the originals on the corporate server. She passed by the printer to pick up the copies on the way to Chris' office.

"I think we are ready," she says as she pulls up a chair. "Lisa is standing by; she will bind it into a professional-looking portfolio when we give her the go-ahead. She needs fifteen minutes; we have an hour and a half to make any changes."

"I've added a copy of the police report and evidence submitted by Monahan. In it, he stated his CPA found several checks missing from the paid invoice file. The bank had electronic copies; all were made payable to and cashed by Darla. According to the CPA, there is evidence that she used a check-writing scheme to issue checks to herself without the knowledge of Lark. If true, it's a clever scheme, except she forgot or didn't know the bank retained electronic copies of all checks and printed them on the monthly statement."

"Chris, we'll need to brainstorm a way to defend this rather damaging evidence. I'm sure we will get a copy of every check and the invoices when the prosecutor provides his discovery. It will be interesting to see if there are any holes in their case."

Amanda and Chris meet with Davis III. Methodically, they go through the portfolio, answering his questions along the way. "Other than the obvious, are there any other obstacles to putting on a good defense for her?" he asks.

Amanda and Chris look at each other knowingly, "Yes," they both say simultaneously.

Amanda takes the lead, "We have a concern that Darla will have a problem with witness credibility. She wears her anger in her voice and her non-verbal communication. Her style doesn't project a soft, innocent demeanor; it's more in your face and suggests a rigid position. She uses her strong personality as a weapon to bully you into her way of thinking. The jury will not like her demeanor and may be offended by her. She will be difficult to manage at the defense table. You will want another lawyer with you to manage, control, and instruct Darla while you focus on the judicial procedures."

Chris adds, "We'll need to do a lot of coaching. We are afraid when the prosecutor starts pushing her; she will fall back into her normal forceful demeanor."

"In the next section, we've listed some questions for Lark Monahan's deposition."

"Impressive," he replies.

Continuing, Amanda inquires, "Will you be at the pretrial hearing, or would you like us to handle it?"

"I don't think both of you need to be at the hearing. Chris, why don't you take the meeting and handle that task about the judge. He has scheduled it for one week from today. I assume we'll be ready."

"Yes, sir, we will."

"Thanks for the great legal work," he continues, "I'll read through your summary and your deposition questions and let you know if I have anything I'd like added. I do want to be present at Lark's deposition. When you are ready, work with Jennie to find a date and time on my calendar." They nod that they understand.

Davis III continues, "I don't think Mr. Monahan would have brought charges against Darla if the amount of money wasn't so large. No business person would want the kind of publicity this is going to create. I'm sure he wants his money if the judge orders restitution. The county prosecutor has taken the matter out of Monahan's hands. It's a criminal case now, and our car dealer is not going to control the outcome."

"I have one more topic of discussion today. It's the kind of discussion I hate to have. You both do great legal work, but the rumor mill in the office has you tagged as not just legal colleagues but also as an office romance. Sorry to say people don't mind their own business; I'm obliged to tell you that the firm frowns on personal relationships that distract from its legal work. While the firm can't dictate what you do on your own time, I'd suggest you avoid intimate dinners or public where others might see you. Your office colleagues have been keeping the rumor mill buzzing about your relationship, which isn't productive for the firm. That said, you are two consenting adults; I leave it to you to manage the perception of whatever it is you are sharing."

Chris sits quietly throughout the monologue; Amanda knows her face is beet red. Chris replies for both, "Sir, you can trust our relationship does not affect our legal contribution and, yes, we will manage the perceptions. Thank you for sharing the partner's concerns." Davis III excuses them with thanks for the exemplary work. They quickly rise from the conference table, exit the room, and return directly to their offices without exchanging words.

Amanda is mortified. She reaches her office and closes the door. Her cell phone alerts her to a text message; it's from Chris. "Ouch, that was unpleasant. I'll fix dinner at my place tonight. Come at six; we can talk then." He adds an emoji heart.

Chapter 15

◇◇◇◇◇◇

She arrives at Chris' apartment, dials his unit number on the door entry system, and hears the buzz that the door is unlocked. As she arrives at his second-floor condo, he hands her a glass of wine and smiles at her. "No partners live in this building. We are okay." She gives him a weak smile and a warm hug. He continues, "That was an amazing meeting until the end."

She smiles, "Yes, it was, but the end put a real damper on the whole experience. I can't believe we've been that obvious; it was embarrassing. For the record, the firm doesn't control my feelings or my desire to spend time with you."

"Ditto! I'm sure Aaron is our rumor monger. He's made several side comments to me. He's sure we are getting special treatment because Davis III selected us for the embezzlement case. There's a little envy. Not only because of Davis III but also because he can't get you to give him a second look."

"He can't get me to give him the first look. But you might be right. He hasn't had a great start with the firm. Now that the partners know about our relationship, we'll keep everything cool and heartless at the office and warm and intimate in our condos. Deal?"

"Deal. Amanda, one more thing, I'm sorry Davis III left you out of the pretrial hearing."

"Chris, I can't tell you how many pretrial hearings I attended when I clerked at the Iowa Supreme Court. More than I can count. Not only do I have the experience, but I, also know Judge Brooks; he's a personal friend of the Chief Justice. I'm okay with Davis III's directive, but it's his loss, as I could have nailed that meeting for the firm. I'll help prepare if you want, but I know you'll do a great job with or without my contribution."

"I will take you up on your offer," he replied, "I always love to learn from those who have experience."

"By the way, I got a message this morning from Jennifer; she found the person who matches CharlesM. It's Charles Myers, my birth father's brother, my uncle. He lives in Marshalltown, where my birth parents grew up, fell in love, and now both live in eternity. I sent him a message before coming over tonight, and he replied immediately. He's invited me to lunch at the Elmwood Country Club in Marshalltown on Saturday. He has agreed to plan an afternoon to get acquainted and tour Marshalltown. His wife is out of town, and since we are strangers, he's suggesting I bring a friend with me. Nice gesture on his part. Would you like to go?"

"Would you like me to go?"

"Yes, I would, and to my knowledge, no partners live in Marshalltown or are members of that country club," she smiles. "Having four ears to listen will be better than two. I don't want to miss anything he might say. We can compare what we've learned on the way home.

"When I sent the message, I was concerned how this total stranger might react to a message out of the blue from a person claiming to be his niece. I certainly don't want to disrupt his life, the memory of his brother, or his privacy, but I would like to know more about what led up to my adoption."

"Let me make arrangements for a rental car. I'll get something classy, not a basic Chevy or Ford. If we're going to a country club, we will go in style. What time do we need to be there?"

"Eleven-thirty Saturday morning. The drive will take us forty-five minutes to an hour. Let's try to leave around ten. I'd also like to stop at the cemetery before returning to Des Moines."

Chris has been jotting notes. "I will make myself useful and research a route that gets us to the country club, then the cemetery, and back to Des Moines." He smiles as she leans forward to give him a thank-you hug and kiss.

Chapter 16

◇◇◇◇◇◇

Saturday morning finally arrives, and as she steps out of the building, she sees Chris waiting beside the rental car. She gives him a broad smile of approval. "A *BMW SUV?* Classy."

He smiles with her delight and approval, opens the passenger door, bows slightly at the waist "your chariot awaits."

The drive to Marshalltown is delightful; the conversation is non-stop. It's like old friends who have traveled together many times. The weather is cooperating; the sun is out, and, for a change, there is no wind. The reflection of the rolling hills and groves of trees whip by the car window in a green blur. Traffic is light, making for a leisurely morning drive. Having Chris behind the wheel adds yet another pleasant view; he is an attractive man.

"Chris, tell me about your family. I know they live

in Minnesota, and your dad owns a custom cabinet business. What does your mother do? What about your siblings? What is the origin of your ancestry?"

"I anticipated that you wouldn't be silent for the hour drive." he chuckles. "I had a great childhood; I've shared that with you before. My dad was always busy at work, and my mother was the perfect wife and mother. She volunteered with the PTA at my school, was active at the country club, our Lutheran church, and was always involved in fundraising events for local not-for-profit charitable organizations. She loves to cook and designed a fabulous kitchen that any gourmet cook would die to have.

"Mom was particularly interested in issues affecting early childhood learning. She was unrelenting when it came to taking full advantage of education. She didn't expect us to get all A's, but she demanded we give our best effort in school. Going to college was required and not negotiable.

"My parents were great role models. I've always known I would not marry until I found a girl like Mom. And now that I've found you, I know that I can replicate the trust, honesty, and love that they exhibited throughout my life." He glances briefly at her in the passenger seat; she's smiling broadly. Mentally she is thinking that she's enjoying the direction their relationship is taking.

"My brother, Ben, graduated from the University of Minnesota. He works with Dad in the business. Ben is a gifted and creative artist with wood. His first contribution was the development of some unique product options for kitchen cabinets that have increased profits. He's engaged to be married; her name is Allysa. I'm sure they will marry within the year.

"My sister, Melissa, is the youngest; she's a sophomore at the University of Minnesota. She's majoring in education and is on a path to being a special education teacher. She's a miniature of my mother, not only in her looks but also in her drive, organizational skills, and her love of early childhood development.

"In terms of my ancestry, the Reed surname is English and Irish. My mother is Swedish, Danish, and Norwegian; thus, our Lutheran church connection. That's about it; that's my family?"

"Your brother, Ben, is in the family business. Why aren't you?"

Chris pauses for a moment, then replies, "I guess I always felt I needed to be successful on my own before I asked my father to bring me into the business. I applied to Drake University because I wanted to make my own way. I did not want to follow the family tradition of going to the U of M. Drake is a smaller school where I felt I would have more involvement opportunities; I knew I wanted to go into law, and Drake has an excellent legal program. At Drake, no one cared that my last name was Reed, and I didn't have to walk in my father's footsteps. My dad provides significant financial support to the U of M and is well-known on campus by the professors and administration.

"Then I discovered I liked Des Moines. I decided to get my feet wet here and prove that I was worthy of a leadership role in our three-generation business. I didn't want to feel that Dad was handing me something because I shared his surname. Ben's different; he doesn't aspire to be at the organization's top; he's happy working at the firm and managing production. I want you to meet my dad and mom; I think you'll like them and the rest of the family."

"I'd like to meet them. I'm ready for a road trip to Minneapolis. Could a visit to the Mall of America and dinner at the Nicollet Island Inn be included in the trip?" she asks, hopefully. "I'll even buy dinner. Speaking of meeting parents, I'd like to take you to Pella."

The Marshalltown exit is just ahead. Thanks to Chris' planning, they drove directly to the Elmwood Country Club. It's an imposing stately white structure. The green awnings on the south side provide a nice contrast to the all-white exterior. As they approach, they can see the covered portico and assume that it is the main entrance. They park and walk around the circular driveway toward the door. Expecting Charles Myers will provide them with a tour of the club, they set aside the temptation to walk around to the south side of the building to enjoy the view.

Approaching the clubhouse, the massive door of this beautiful clubhouse opens, and a tall, attractive, well-dressed man comes forward to greet us. "Welcome to Elmwood Country Club, Amanda Springs. I'm Charles Myers. I can't tell you what a pleasure it is to meet you finally. You've been in my thoughts for twenty-seven years."

Amanda feels a tear slowly dripping down her cheek; she knew this would be an emotional day, but she didn't expect tears to flow because a stranger greets her. "How did you know it was me?"

He chuckles, "Amanda, first you look just like your mother and, second, our club members generally walk around to the south side of the building via that path," he points to a sidewalk on his left that disappears around the building. He continues to smile with the pleasure of meeting her.

"Let me introduce my friend, Christopher Reed. We are colleagues at Helling, Newbiggin, and Sloan and good friends."

Chris reaches his hand out to Charles, "Nice to meet you; call me Chris."

Greetings over; Charles asks them to follow him. He made special arrangements for a private dining room that overlooks the beautiful lush green golf course. The clubhouse sits at the top of the hill, and the golf course rolls down the valley as a stunning backdrop. There is a row of brightly colored chairs surrounding the final green, and Charles explains that the chairs have been a constant for many years and have become somewhat of a logo for the club.

Charles opens a door and holds it for them to go through. As her eyes adjust from the bright sunlight to the dimly lit room, she sees photo albums lined up on the credenza on the far wall and a white cloth-draped round table with four upholstered high back chairs in the center of an elegantly furnished room. She turns and sees that the view out the window is breathtaking.

"Can I offer you a drink?" he asks as he leads them to a bar sitting in the corner of the room.

"Just water for me now, maybe a glass of wine with lunch."

Chris and Charles each have a cold beer. "Let's get comfortable at the table and order our lunch; then tell me how you found me."

Charles explains that Elmwood has recently hired a new chef, Kurt, and everything on the menu is delicious. "You won't be disappointed with anything you order." An attractive young college-aged male takes their order and closes the door as he leaves.

Amanda begins the conversation, "I've known since I was a child that I was adopted. My parents gave me children's books when I was young. The characters in the books were young, happy girls, told by their parents that they were "not expected, but were selected." She assures Charles that she always felt loved, secure, and wanted by her parents. Her everyday life was as normal as any natural-born child. She explained, "I had a traditional small-town childhood in a tightly woven family. I have two brothers; I love all the family events and the Dutch traditions of my hometown."

Amanda asks Charles, "Have you met Tom Graves, your brother's attorney?"

"Yes, I know him quite well; I met him after the accident, but now, I see him in Iowa City regularly."

"I had lunch with Tom several weeks ago; he gave me the DNA test kits and let me know I would find the DNA results for my birth father and birth mother on both AncestryDNA and 23andMe. And, of course, I did."

Amanda continues, "I applied to an organization called Search Angels and was contacted by Jennifer, one of their volunteers. The DNA showed that I share solid DNA with three males on my birth father's side, CharlesM, MichaelS, and AdamJ. Jennifer thinks it's two Uncles and a brother." Charles raises an eyebrow, says nothing, and continues to listen.

"Jennifer sent me the obituary of your father, Dr. George K Myers; it stated he had two sons, Charles Myers and Robert Myers. Jennifer discovered on the internet that you were the older brother and were still living in Marshalltown. That's when I sent you the note through the Ancestry messaging system.

"Tom Graves told me that Bob and MaryAnne did their DNA hoping my twin sister and I would find them. Jennifer has no clue about the two other male siblings." One listed his name only as MichaelS. Since the obituary named you as my only Uncle, Jennifer and I are confused by the strong centimorgan connection of Michael. The second male is a full brother. Based on the obituary, I'm assuming that's Adam, and my biological parents had him after they married in 2005." She pauses to get his reaction.

Charles responds, "I did submit my DNA as Bob requested, but I've never bothered to look at the results. When I got the message that the results were in, I sent Bob my usernames and passwords. It was his research. I wanted to meet my twin nieces and hoped he would be successful, but I wasn't into the DNA stuff.

"Bob and Mary Anne did have a son, Adam, he's fifteen. I'm his legal guardian, and that's why my wife is in Iowa City. I've owned my CPA firm in Marshalltown for many years, but I can work from anywhere. With video teleconferencing, email, electronic signatures, and other new technologies, being in two places at once can be relatively easy. When my brother died, I opened a small office in Iowa City; I needed a place to work each day.

"We split our time between Marshalltown and Iowa City. Jill and I are committed to caring for Adam, and I will commute until he graduates from high school. After the accident, we thought it would be mentally healthy for Adam to stay in his family home and continue to go to school with his friends. In three years, when Adam goes to college, we can choose where to live. We like the college town feel of Iowa City, but our roots and lifelong friends are here in Marshalltown. For me, being Adam's guardian has been a blessing; I love him like the son I never had. Would you like to meet him?"

Amanda assured him that she would.

"I will need time to prepare him for this next surprise in his life; I've never told him about the twins, and I don't know if his parents did."

Charles continues, "Now, this Michael DNA match

is all new information, and it's pretty strange. What does your Jennifer say about him?"

Chris takes the lead, "Actually, it was Amanda who took the initiative to send a message to Michael. She learned that he lives in a suburb of Seattle. Michael had just learned through his DNA results that the father who raised him is not his biological father. But the mother who raised him is his biological mother. He's frankly stunned by the news and is trying to determine how his two siblings are natural-born children of their parents, but he's not. By your reaction, we can assume you don't know either."

Charles remained silent, but a flash of something crossed his face suggesting he might have had a flashback to an old memory. It was so brief that Chris wondered if he had imagined it.

"Nevertheless, DNA doesn't lie, and there is another close male relative to you and your brother."

"Is my grandmother, your mother, still living?" Amanda inquires.

"Yes, she is; let's hold that conversation. I want to show you this first." Charles gets up, walks to the credenza, and returns with a scrapbook. "As part of your private adoption, your adoptive father agreed to send annual pictures and a report about your health and well-being." Charles hands her the book. "Robert found this about six years ago in our dad's office." She opens the scrapbook; familiar images appear. They are in chronological order from birth until she graduated from high school. Her father had sent her birth grandfather an annual report with a current school picture, local newspaper clippings, and a hand-written note.

The tears stream down her face. Charles hands her a crisp, clean handkerchief from the front pocket of his blazer. "I think my brother would want you to have this scrapbook." She smiles through the tears and thanks him for this treasure. Knowing that her birth father had touched every page, she gently moves her hand across the cream-colored paper as she thinks how he might have felt finding this secret hidden in his father's desk. She feels close to her father as she caresses each page.

The waiter arrived with their order as Charles was rising to refresh their drinks. Amanda requests a glass of chardonnay; both Chris and Charles have the same. Throughout the delicious lunch, the conversation continues to flow.

"You were conceived when I was 20 years old. I remember the whole drama and my father's unrelenting anger. My brother was upset and angry in his bedroom, and my mother was crying uncontrollably in hers. I'd never heard my mother cry before that day; even at 20, it wasn't a comfortable situation. Dad went back and forth between the two bedrooms yelling at one and then the other.

"Dad then called our family attorney and arranged for him to come to the house the next day. His next call was to MaryAnne's dad demanding that they bring MaryAnne to meet with the attorney. He returned to the bedrooms, instructed his wife to control herself, and explained to Bob that the attorney, the Blancs, and the family would meet the next day. He made it clear that Bob had better damn well be there. Dad, of course, excluded me from their meeting, but I heard every word through the walls."

"This must have been as traumatic for you as it was for your brother and his girlfriend. I heard from Tom Graves that MaryAnne's parents sent her to Minnesota to live with an aunt. He said your brother could not persuade her parents to tell him where she was living."

"Yes, that's true. Dad was not a force to be challenged; they didn't want any more threats from him. They never told Bob where she was living or what happened during or after the delivery. Eventually, Bob stopped asking and reluctantly continued with his life. He didn't know there were twin girls until he reconnected with MaryAnne ten years later."

"Charles, my DNA indicates that I have two half-sisters on my birth mother's side; these girls do not share any DNA with your brother. That, according to Jennifer, means MaryAnne conceived them with another man. From the obituary, I found their names, Brittany and Kayla. Do you know anything about them?"

"Wow, Amanda, I can't imagine how you've been able to deal with all these recently discovered relatives. MaryAnne did have two daughters, and my brother isn't their biological father. When they married in 2005, he immediately started adoption proceedings and made them part of his legal family, and he loved and treated them as his own."

"Do you know where they are living? And if they would be receptive to meeting me?"

"Amanda, the answer is—yes and no. Yes, I know where they live, but I don't know if they'd like to meet you. The older one, Brittainy, graduated from college, is married, and has a child of her own. She is living in Wisconsin. The younger daughter, Kayla, graduated from college and is now living in California. She's still grieving the loss of her parents and is somewhat of a lost soul. I'll contact both of them and see if they are willing to meet their new half-sister."

"Can you tell me about MaryAnne; when, where, and by whom did she give birth to two daughters?" Do you know if her parents are still living?"

With a sigh, he appeared to be thinking about how to respond. After a long pause in the conversation, Charles finally replies. "You know, that's not my story to tell. I think Brittany might be willing to share what she knows about her mother's history and the events of her life, but I'm not sure about Kayla; she's pretty protective of her mother's memory."

"What an amazing day! I'm anxious to learn more about my birth mother and her parents. I hope Brittany is open to that discussion."

Chapter 17

◇◇◇◇◇◇

Amanda's head is spinning. "So, let me recap. Charles, you are my biological uncle; I have a twin sister and a fifteen-year-old brother, Adam. I have two half-sisters, daughters of my birth mother, and my birth father adopted them. And then, there is another uncle, Michael, who you've never heard of."

"Amanda, you sound like the lawyer you are. That was an exact summation of the facts."

"Do I have any other relatives? Did my birth mother have siblings? Do I have any aunts or uncles or cousins?" Amanda inquires.

"That I can answer, MaryAnne was an only child. I've often wondered how she and her parents survived the difficulties of 1993. Their only daughter was pregnant at sixteen, and the birth father's family rejected her. Imagine the pain of knowing that your actions to approve the adoption caused you to lose your first grandchild, or in their situation, their first two granddaughters. It must have been hard for them. Unfortunately, my aristocratic, domineering father deemed MaryAnne to be 'from the wrong side of town,' and he wasn't about to allow his vision of success for his son to be destroyed by an unexpected, undesirable event. I've often wondered if it had been the bank president's daughter if Dad would have rejected his granddaughters."

"You are not complimentary about your father, Charles. Is there more to this story of a medical doctor fulfilling his image as God?"

Charles chuckles, "You've never met him, and you've described him perfectly. Let's leave my father for a discussion on another day. I'm enjoying this chicken caesar salad and don't want to ruin my appetite." Her instincts tell her she has much more to learn about her grandfather, but now is, obviously, not the time. She makes a mental note to follow up with some research on Dr. George Myers, the successful obstetrician from Marshalltown.

Charles gets up and retrieves two photo albums. "Here are two more albums for you to take home. The first is Bob, growing up in elementary, junior high, and high school. You'll find pictures of MaryAnne at some of the early high school dances and proms. The second album covers Bob's college life; education consumed him both in learning and later as a professor at the University. I think you'll enjoy his life through these pictures. They are yours to keep and to share with your twin sister when you find her."

"Thank you, Charles; I can't tell you how much this means to me."

"Charles, what can you tell Amanda about her twin sister? There is no DNA for her in any of the test results. Do you know where she lives? Does she know she was adopted? Does she know she has a twin?" Charles raises both hands in front of his body as a gesture to stop the questions.

"I'm sorry, Chris and Amanda, I don't know anything, but I can tell you with certainty that you have a twin, and my brother and his wife were looking for your sister before the accident. They even hired a private detective to try to find her. When she was born, she was named Emma. But like you, her name could have been changed by the adoptive parents."

Amanda wonders aloud, "If my twin hasn't done DNA, and we don't know her adoptive name or where she lives, how in the world can I find her?"

"Amanda, it seems like an impossible task. It will be a demanding search, just as it was for my brother and his wife." He withdraws a business card from his pocket. "Here's the name and telephone number for their private detective. He's still on retainer; please feel free to contact him."

"Thank you." Rising from his chair, Charles suggests they move along. Let me give you a quick tour of the country club. Your great-great-grandfather was one of the original founding members of the club. Our family has held continuous membership for all one hundred and twenty-five years." He walks them down the hall to a majestic staircase that brings them to the upper level. They arrive near the entrance to the main dining room and the south porch. Walking past the bar and through the beautiful grand ballroom, they agreed it was an elegant facility. Out the door, they find themselves under the portico where they first met Charles two hours ago.

"Amanda, would you like to visit the cemetery?" They walk down the circular drive and head to the parking lot. "I thought you might want to see the burial location for your birth parents."

Chris has been quiet through most of the conversation but finds his voice, "Charles, that would be great. Amanda mentioned that she wanted to walk the cemetery and find the gravesite. With you as our guide, it will make it much easier and save us a lot of time."

With a nod, Charles suggests, "Leave your car here, and I'll bring you back. My SUV is the gray one on the left."

While Amanda is contemplating all that she's heard, Chris asks if she'd like to be in the front to chat with her uncle or if she'd like the back seat to be somewhat alone. She slips into the backseat. After closing her car door, Chris secures his seatbelt on the front passenger side and engages Charles with questions about the country club, Marshalltown, and his work.

Amanda is thankful that she's been left alone and

allowed time to reflect on her newfound family. She opens the photo album of the high school years and looks page by page at his accomplishments both in academics and sports. Turning the pages, Amanda sees her birth mother dressed in a tea-length rose-colored evening dress. They are standing together under an arch of paper mache flowers. She's beautiful. She's gazing up a Robert, and the look in her eyes is unconditional happiness and love. Amanda sighs deeply and regrets that she never got to meet them.

The drive to the cemetery doesn't take long, but then again, anywhere in Marshalltown can be reached within ten minutes. Charles drives through the cemetery and stops at an impressive mausoleum with Myers engraved on the considerable-sized rectangle base. Gesturing out the front car window, Charles explains, "Our ancestors invested in this location, purchasing fifty individual plots for family internments. I guess they wanted their family around them for eternity." Pointing at the mausoleum, he continues, "Burial of the older ancestors was above ground. When family deaths fully occupied that structure, the burial of descendants started filling the surrounding plots. This area of the cemetery is called 'Myers' Corner' by the locals."

Amanda remains silent in the back seat. When Charles kills the car engine, she opens the car door and walks reflectively by the various Myers' granite markers. Amanda finds the tombstones for Robert and MaryAnne Myers in a tranquil area under the shade of a large oak tree. She notices that they have been buried a considerable distance from his father, Dr. George Myers, and wonders who selected their burial location.

"Charles, thank you for bringing us here. For me, it's as though this place has filled a void in my soul. Just being near their grave brings—I don't know how to describe it—perhaps peace and fulfillment is the best way to explain my feelings."

"It was my pleasure. Please, let's stay in contact with each other. I will talk with Adam, Brittany, and Kayla and explain the shared DNA. I'll see if I can arrange a meeting with them, and I hope if you find any information on Michael in Seattle, that you will share it with me." She assures him she will stay in touch.

Solemnly, Charles says, "Amanda, I have one final question." Amanda turns and looks him in the eye and waits.

Slowly he forms his question. "Amanda, at lunch, you asked if my mother, your grandmother, was still living. I told you she was but didn't provide any additional information. Toni Myers, your grandmother, is seventy-five years old but acts more like sixty. She still lives in the original family home here in Marshalltown and would like to meet you.

"She remembers holding you and your sister just after you were born. For the two days before being transferred to the care of your adoptive parents, she cared for you. She has thought of you for these past twenty-seven years. She was considering coming to the country club today but didn't feel it was appropriate. She asked me to invite you to stop for tea this afternoon. Now, I need to stop babbling. Amanda, would you like to meet your grandmother?"

Chapter 18

◇◇◇◇◇◇◇

Michael approaches his mother's house with a bit of hesitation and some reluctance. Matt says that the only way to resolve the mystery revealed by his DNA results is to talk with his mother. Wanda has the key to unlocking the mystery of why his birth father is someone other than Harold, who raised him.

Over and over in his mind, he rehearses the questions he wants to ask, but each question causes a red hue to move up from his neck to his face. He's embarrassed to be asking his mother about her sex life. As a young boy, when he first learned about the birds and the bees, he wanted to imagine that they only did it four times in their life, one for each of their children; okay, now it's only three times since Mom was not with Dad for my conception.

Mom was delighted when I wanted to come over

for a visit. I can only hope she will feel the same when I leave. The middle of the afternoon when Dad would still be at work seemed like a perfect time. He wanted this to be a private conversation between mother and son and hoped to persuade her not to share it with Dad, Megan, or Matt.

Driving down the familiar street, he sees the family home ahead on the right; memories of his childhood flood through the windshield. He remembered his friends playing soccer out in the street and staying up late every night during the summer until it was too dark to continue. It was a great childhood. Our parents didn't have to worry about us, it was a safe neighborhood, and the riots and disruptions that are common today did not invade our tranquil lives.

There, in the front yard, is the old tree. We built the treehouse when I was nine. Matt and I spent hours there and were the envy of the other neighborhood boys. Here's where we learned about sex; one friend was a doctor's son, and he had access to some fantastic books. He borrowed them, not, of course, with his father's knowledge. He would find a good book, then stuff it down his pants to get out of the house without being discovered. Racing to the treehouse, he only stopped to breathe when he was sure he'd made a clean getaway. Michael smiles as he remembers sitting shoulder to shoulder with a flashlight to look at the pictures and try to understand why anyone would want to have intercourse.

He unbuckles the seat belt and pulls himself out

of the car. As he turns toward the house, his mother comes sprinting across the yard to greet him. She is there with a loving hug and expresses her pleasure at seeing her son home for the afternoon.

"Come in, come in. I have some ice tea made. I can't wait to hear what you've been up to and the reason you are visiting today. Michael, I'm glad to see you, but it's the middle of the day, and you never come except on weekends or when we plan special family celebrations."

They moved through the familiar hallway to the back of the house, stopped in the kitchen for the ice tea pitcher and two glasses, and headed for the Adirondack chairs on the enclosed four-season porch. Once seated, she didn't waste a minute, "OK, Micky, you have my undivided attention, spill your guts, why are you here."

"Micky? You haven't called me that for years," he said to stall a little. She waited with a smile and a look of unconditional love. Swallowing his nerves, Michael launched himself into his planned speech, "You know Matt has a passion for genealogy. He's stitched our family ancestors together, but he wants more than just the paper trail. A new venture using DNA is his current passion for adding to his collection of dead ancestors. Now he's looking for some of the living ones."

Her chin dropped just a little, and the smile waned; this was not what she was expecting to hear.

Ignoring the confused look on her face, "He called me a couple of months ago and asked if I would participate in his project by doing an AncestryDNA test. He wanted a close relative to do the test so he could do something called 'triangulate' us with other DNA matches. Megan participated. too."

"Yes, I remember his enthusiasm for getting DNA tests done by the whole family. Your dad and I decided not to be his guinea pigs. It's a new technology, and we just weren't sure of the ramifications of making our DNA available to others. We've seen on television some of the shows where they can use it to solve murders. Sorry, I'm going off on a tangent."

"Yes, it is a new technology, and I know Matt is over the moon excited about his new venture. But I'm sorry now that I agreed to spit in the tube for him."

"Why?" she inquired. She locked her eyes on mine, her confusion visible on her face.

"I don't know how to start this conversation, Mom. Please, let me tell you without interruption. I probably will stumble and do this poorly, but it's not a conversation I ever expected to have with my mother."

"Now you have my attention; okay, I'll be quiet, no interruptions and no questions until you're through."

"Mom, the DNA indicates that Dad is not my biological father and that you had sex with another man; his name is George Myers." Mom's jaw dropped open, and I'm sure it hit the floor, but she didn't interrupt. "This Myers is my biological father. I'm more than stunned by the facts revealed in my DNA test, but I absolutely cannot imagine any scenario that would explain how you became pregnant by a man in Iowa."

Mom sat there for several minutes without uttering a single word. He could see in her eyes that her brain was processing the bombshell he had just dropped. It was unclear whether she was trying to build a defense for her actions, trying to come up with an excuse, or she was searching her memory to determine how what he just said could be true.

Finally, her eyes found his, and in no uncertain terms, she said with conviction, "Michael, I have no idea what you are talking about; none. None whatsoever." she stated emphatically. The color rises from her neck to her face, and he realizes his accusations genuinely mortified her. "There has to be a mistake in the DNA results."

"Mom, DNA does not lie; I don't have any DNA match to Dad, and my shared matches with Megan and Matt show that I'm their half-brother."

After a drink of her tea to moisten her dry mouth, she expelled a long sigh and then began her confession. "When we were young, your father and I were college students at Iowa State University. We were married in Ames, but I swear I never had sex with anyone but your father. He is my soulmate and the love of my life. Michael, I would never do such a thing to him or me." The tears were welling in her eyes, but she held them in check. It was easy to see that she was hurt and upset by my comments and conclusions.

"After our marriage, we were both eager to start a family. I was having problems getting pregnant, and we eventually went to a fertility specialist. The doctor put me on some fertility drugs. After months of trying and failing to get pregnant, the doctor instructed your dad to collect a sperm sample and place it into a vial with a unique solution to boost the sperm. The following day, I went to his clinic. The doctor injected your dad's boosted sperm into me. We were thrilled when I missed my next menstrual cycle and then another. The doctor confirmed I was pregnant.

"When I was in my fourth month, your dad got an offer to be an engineer at Boeing in Seattle. We were excited—a new career, a new home, and our firstborn due in five months. We packed up the few household items we had and headed to Washington in a U-Haul truck. You were born here in Seattle, then Matt and Megan followed without further fertility intervention."

"Mom, someone duped you; I don't think the doctor returned Dad's sperm to your body. What was this doctor's name? Where did he practice? He used the sperm of another man for your intrauterine insemination."

His mother sat stunned. He reached over and removed the tea glass from her hand and set it carefully on the table. "No, Michael, I don't believe that. You are our first-born son, and your father and I are your parents."

"Mom, you are my parents; I love you both, and I love the life we've shared. No one could have had a better childhood. But my DNA isn't Dad's."

"Michael, this is not what I expected to hear today. I expected you were coming over to tell me that you and

Janey were finally getting engaged," she smiles weakly. "Please, don't say anything to your father, Matt or Megan, and let me wrap my head around what you've said. I need to come to grips with it first before I can figure out what to say to your dad and what should be done about it if what you say is true."

"Mum's the word. I'm sorry, Mom. We've always been honest with each other, and I knew there had to be some explanation for this DNA surprise. And Mom, more bad news, Janey and I split up about three weeks ago. I'm sorry to be this bearer of bad news."

They sat for another hour, talking about family plans, his job, and distant relatives. As he started to rise from the porch chair to leave, she grabbed his arm, pulled him into her embrace, and quietly said, "Michael, I love you, and I'm telling you the truth."

Chapter 19

◇◇◇◇◇◇

Standing in the North Hill Cemetery, viewing the family's impressive mausoleum, Amanda contemplates her uncle's question: *Is she interested in meeting her biological grandmother?* She mentally considered the pros and cons. Why not? What possible harm could come from a visit with her? She smiles at Chris, inquiring if he is willing to take more time? He smiles and nods, letting her know the decision is hers.

"Yes, Charles, I would like to meet my grandmother."

"Mom was hoping you would agree to see her. I will call and let her know we are on our way. Make yourselves comfortable in the Lexus; I won't be but a minute." Charles walks farther into the cemetery for a private conversation with his mother. He returns quickly and moves in behind the wheel. He circles the pond finding his way back to the front gate.

"Our family home is one of the oldest in Marshalltown; it's near the downtown area. Just one block off Main Street and within walking distance to church, the bank, the courthouse; well, you get the picture, everything is just a hop, skip, and a jump away for Mom's daily excursions. Her car is only used for a weekly drive to the country club or occasionally when she volunteers at the hospital. Over the years, she has accepted volunteer activities that are within walking distance. Location matters to her."

Charles continues his monologue, providing more information about his family home. "The family lived on the second floor, and Dad used the first floor for his medical practice. Patients would enter from the front brick porch into the waiting room; it was an elegant living room with a warm fireplace. The first-floor arrangement made the patients feel comfortable and at ease before and after seeing the doctor in the examination rooms. The nurse's station was under the staircase just inside the front door, and it was extended into the hallway by the nurse each morning to block anyone from passing down the hall without her knowledge." He smiles as he recalls the memory.

"All that has changed now; Mom remodeled the house when Dad died. She's created a comfortable home, upstairs and down. Unfortunately, she's alone most of the time except for occasional visits by her family."

He draws their attention to various points of interest. "My best friend still lives in this old house; this is

Elks Park where Robert and I played basketball, and there's Rogers Elementary School. The school is only one block from our house; we walked every day regardless of the weather."

As he turns the corner, he says, "Mom keeps everything neat, tidy, and well maintained, especially if you compare her property to others in this old neighborhood. The walkway leading to the house is unusual; instead of being perpendicular to the street, it's diagonal. As you can see, it leads out the front steps right to the corner of the intersecting streets; peculiar, but it sort of fits the house, its location, and its prior use as a medical clinic."

On the elaborate wrap-around porch is an attractive, well-dressed, physically fit woman; Charles waves and shouts, "Hello, Mom, are you ready for company?" A cloth draped, round table on the porch has a beautiful vase of multicolored roses; probably, freshly cut from her garden. Waiting on a sideboard table is a silver tea service and miniature bite-size cakes. She's amazed that her grandmother could put this all together at a moment's notice; she must have expected we would accept her invitation and prepared all of this in advance. Amanda is glad she put on a lovely summer dress for this trip; it certainly is appropriate for her grandmother's unexpected tea party.

"Hello, welcome to the Myers Mansion," she chuckles. "Can you imagine an old lady like me living alone in this old relic of a house?"

Amanda extends her hand and introduces herself

and Chris, "I think your home looks lovely, Mrs. Myers. You must spend a great deal of time working in your flower beds. They are overflowing with a kaleidoscope of color and greenery. I'm afraid I didn't inherit any of your genes for growing lush, beautiful plants. I've never had a green thumb."

"The plants are my friends; I talk with them each day, prune here, snip there and ensure they are happy and well-fed. They return the favor with a glorious frame to the house and, as you can see, decorations for my table," her hand sweeps our attention to the vase of roses.

She leads them to the table, invites everyone to sit as she carefully serves tea from the heavy silver teapot. She has done this for years, as she gracefully accomplishes the task without spilling a drop. Placing a tray of petits fours on the table, she signals that all is ready for their get-acquainted conversation.

Lowering herself gracefully into her chair, she begins, "I am pleased that you agreed to visit today. I was thinking about driving out to the country club to surprise you. You probably noticed the table was set for four and not three. I decided that coming without your prior approval would be not only unladylike but also rude. I asked Charles to find a way to invite you here. You must have a million questions, but let me start with a little story then I will answer any questions you have." She pauses briefly, and Amanda nods her head in agreement.

"My son, Robert was intellectually brilliant; he was

a voracious reader. Education and studying were a pleasure for him, not a chore. He was active in school, playing basketball, football, and baseball, and was well-liked by his classmates and teachers," she sighs at the memory. "He served as the class president, had leads in the school drama productions, and was homecoming king his senior year. There was no question he was going to amount to something special as an adult. His father and I laid the groundwork for both our boys to be successful.

"But in 1993, the wheels came off the track. Our son knew better but forgot that having unprotected sex was like playing Russian roulette. His high school sweetheart got pregnant, and it was a dreadful scene for days and even months. George, my husband, was unduly dramatic, which made matters worse. MaryAnne, bless her heart, endured a great deal of anger and insults from George. Her parents sent her to live with an aunt, and my husband threatened Robert with dire consequences if he looked for her. To say that the relationship between my son and my husband was tense is an understatement. Robert loved MaryAnne, and he never forgave his father for his severe threats of disinheritance and his unwillingness to pay for his college education if he disobeyed. The two rarely spoke to each other after that event, and my husband died still estranged from his son."

"I'm sorry to hear that; it must have been difficult for all of you. Can you tell me anything about my birth mother during that time? How did her parents react?"

"MaryAnne's mother, Gabrielle Blanc, and I were

close friends before 1993 when George forbade me to continue our friendship. While the *good* doctor was busy with his patients, she and I would sneak out to meet at the park and cry on each other's shoulders. Gaby was devastated by what was happening to her family and her daughter. As for MaryAnne, she was living in St. Cloud, Minnesota with Gaby's sister."

"Do you know if my maternal grandparents are still living?"

Toni looks to her son, "Have you given her information on how to contact Brittainy? She's the person to be telling the Blanc family side of this story."

"I'm contacting Brittainy this week to see if she is open to a conversation with Amanda."

Without answering yes or no to her question, her grandmother continues with her story. "I arrived in Minnesota the day you were born; I was the courier sent by George to take you back to Marshalltown. MaryAnne's parents signed an agreement giving George the legal authority to handle all the adoption details. It upset his plans when twins were born; he already had your adoptive parents lined up to raise one baby. When it became clear he wasn't going to tell them about the twin sister, well, you can imagine the argument we had. I argued that you and your twin should, at least, have the opportunity to be raised together. He wouldn't listen to me or anyone. He went forward with a private adoption for you, never telling the Springs that there were twins. The next day he was in Des Moines placing Emma up for adoption."

Amanda nods her head. "That explains why I found no adoption records in St. Cloud." She makes a mental note to call the Des Moines Social Services on Monday morning.

"MaryAnne didn't want to give either of you up for adoption, but she had no choice; she was only sixteen years old. She was devastated when her mother told her that the twins were separated and adopted by two different families. She was angry with her parents, with George, and then with life in general. She reportedly cried herself to sleep for days after you were born."

Chris had a puzzled look and inquired, "Why didn't they return to a normal father and son relationship? I understand that a father would be disappointed with a son who gets a girl pregnant, but time generally mends those wounds. I know my dad and I would have real knock-down-drag-out arguments, but I knew he loved me. We would always talk it out and reconcile after a day or two."

Charles interceded, "It's a long, complicated story. Dad wasn't an easy man to know or love." Sounding like that was the end of the discussion about Dr. George Myers, they all raised from the table, commenting on the beautiful weather and the pleasant day.

After a tour of the first level of this beautiful home, Amanda suggested that it was time to retrieve their car for the return trip to Des Moines. "Before we leave, may I ask one other question? I'm pursuing my family tree because Robert directed his attorney to provide me with DNA test kits. The results of my DNA show another close Myers relative; his name is Michael, and he lives in Seattle. Michael shared in a text message that his DNA indicates that the man who raised him is not his biological father. Any idea who he is or what his relationship might be to your family?"

The quick flash of something in her eyes and the knowing look she gave Charles was telling; they knew something they weren't sharing. Out of her grandmother's mouth came only these words, "Not a clue."

"Thank you for coming, Amanda. I appreciate your willingness to come for tea today, especially since it was on the spur of the moment. I hope you'll consider returning to Marshalltown and spending more time." Hugs all around, and then they were off to the country club.

En route, Amanda probed for some answers, "Charles, when Chris asked about Michael at luncheon, you had a brief curious look on your face. It just happened again on the porch with your mother. I feel there's something in the past that you might be remembering. Is there anything you could share that would explain Micheal's DNA connection?"

She paused, waiting; she was not going to be the next one to talk. The ball was in his court, and he needed to serve up whatever he would share. They drove several blocks in silence when he suddenly pulled the car to the curb, moved the gear knob into park, and turned to lock eyes with me.

"You are a smart one, and, just like my brother, you

are skilled at reading non-verbal communications. It is a skill that must be valuable for you as an attorney. Without going into the sordid details, let me say my father was a gynecologist. He specialized in infertility treatment and intrauterine insemination. He successfully worked with hundreds of women having difficulty getting pregnant. As you stated earlier, he thought he was God and could do anything. Buying sperm from the viral, good-looking guys at Robert's fraternity house provided him with a source to solve his patient's problems. Robert was furious when he learned about it from one of his fraternity brothers. Sounds far-fetched, I know, but in those early days, gynecologists would frequently walk down the halls at a medical school to find a person with the right genetic makeup to provide sperm for infertility treatment. They would find the right look and build and approach the selected medical student and buy their sperm. Unethical doctors, who thought they were God, would sometimes use their own.

"It was a highly controversial practice, as you might imagine. My grandfather found out about his son's deceptive practices, confronted him, demanded that he discontinue his fertility practice and stick to prenatal care and delivering babies. Dr. George refused his father, calling him 'old-fashioned' and 'out of touch.' Grandpa handled the situation in a way that was under his control. He cut George out of the family fortune and executed a generation-skipping trust. When grandpa died, Robert and I became financially well-heeled. Dad blew a gasket when he learned his father had cut him out. He hired more attorneys than you can shake a stick at but could never reverse the terms of the legally drawn trust. Dad died in 2002; a lonely man. It's not been easy living in this family."

Turning around, he put the car in gear and pulled away from the curb. They drove the remaining distance in silence. Arriving at the country club, Charles helped Amanda out of the car and gave her an enormous hug. "Sorry to say your grandfather was not the citizen of the year, but the rest of the family is quite normal. I'd love to invite you back to Marshalltown for the few family gatherings we have each year. I'll send you a text or call you after I talk with your brother and sisters and see what I can do to arrange a meeting."

Amanda let her smile show in her eyes, "Charles, it has been a pleasure to meet you. Thank you for sharing your family memories. It has been an enlightening, informative, and emotionally charged day."

"Amanda, please drive safely back to Des Moines; we Myers are an anxious bunch when family members are on the road."

Chapter 20

The conversation from Marshalltown was non-stop. They discussed their impressions of the luncheon with Charles and Amanda's overwhelming and unexplainable feeling of closeness to her birth parents.

"I wasn't surprised when Charles shared the depth of George's medical procedures and the length he would go to appear successful," Chris shared. "What wasn't said says volumes about the secrets of old Dr. George. If he lived today with unlimited consumer access to DNA testing, he would be more than worried about his reputation and status as 'Doctor God.' It is unfathomable the damage he may have caused over the years of his practice. How many adults living today could do a DNA test and trace their genetic results back to Marshalltown? George's medical practice would be a case we wouldn't want to defend in court."

Amanda chimes in, "More stunning was that his father bypassed him and gave all his wealth to his grandsons. It spoke volumes to how disgusted my great-grandfather was about my grandfather's professional behavior. I wondered if my great-grandfather was also a doctor. Being a doctor calls for unwavering value to ethics in the medical profession. I can't imagine what else this doctor could have done with his female patients. Ugly to even think about it."

They both agreed on the brighter side that grandmother Toni was a delight. She might be living in the past with the big house and its old-victorian prestige, but she's a pretty youthful seventy-five-year-old. Charles shared that she likes to have Adam spend weekends in Robert's childhood bedroom. Adam reminds her of Robert at that same age. They both agree Toni must be lonely in that big house by herself.

"By the way, Amanda, I think you skillfully asked your grandmother about Michael's relationship to the family. By first sharing that Michael learned his father wasn't his biological father, you made it clear that you weren't accusing her of having an out-of-wedlock son. By not mentioning that the centimorgans indicated he's your half-uncle, you didn't suggest that her husband had had an affair. Well done, counselor."

"Thank you. I started asking the question and then realized the implications of what I was saying. Toni didn't seem to react negatively to the question or seem put out by it."

Changing the direction of the conversation, Amanda offered, "I think I am going to like my half-sister, Brittany. Charles shared that she calls her grandmother once or twice each month, and she occasionally drives from Wisconsin with her daughter, Laura, to spend a night or two in the old family home."

"Kayla is too far away in California to have much of a relationship," Chris reflects. "It's nice that the girls stay in touch with their grandmother."

"I wonder about my birth mother. Neither Charles nor Toni wanted to discuss the subject. Charles said, 'it wasn't his story to tell.' Toni changed the subject and ignored my question."

"Yes, they were secretive, but possibly they feel Brittainy and Kayla should be the ones sharing their mother's story."

Tomorrow is Sunday, it is supposed to be a day of rest, but they agree that they need to spend the day in the office finalizing the recommendation on Darla's embezzlement case. But breakfast at Louie's Wine Dine will still be their first stop.

As they entered Chris' condo, he reached for her hand, leading her to his bed. "I've been thinking about this moment all day," he smiles. He gently lifts her sundress over her head. Her smooth skin excites his senses as he runs his fingers over her breast and down her stomach. He feels the quiver of desire in her body. He pulls her gently toward him and, with utter abandon, feels the need to have her close around him. He gently caresses her, and their lovemaking is sensual, tender, and unbelievably enjoyable. "Amanda, you are a surprising woman, and I love everything about you."

With an exhale of her breath, she replies, "I know." Both settle into a warm, comfortable embrace and immediately fall into a deep satisfying sleep.

They wake the following day surprised that they both slept like the dead. It's nine o'clock in the morning, and they are just now seeing the light of day. Amanda, thankful that she left a toothbrush, gets up and showers, using Chris' body and face wash. Same clothes as yesterday and no makeup will have to do. Off to Louie's for breakfast. Their favorite table in a dimly lit corner just to the right of the entrance is open and available. They order their usual breakfast and start talking about work. They eat quickly, text for an Uber, and arrive at their office.

As they review the prosecutor's witness list and discovery documents, a red flag goes up in Amanda's mind. One of the names on the prosecutor's list was familiar to her. She digs through her notes. "Chris, we have a problem," pointing at the witness list, "this is one of Darla's former employers. I tried to talk with her last week. She was evasive when I called, and I thought she might have more to say, but she wouldn't divulge anything. Obviously, she had something to say, and she said it to the prosecutor. The prosecutor is calling her to testify that Darla was dishonest in a previous job as a bookkeeper. Davis III is not going to be happy that she possibly lied to us."

"Let's get an appointment after Lark's deposition

tomorrow. We need to express our concerns. We both know Darla will not be a likable or creditable witness, and now the prosecutor has a former employer testifying that this wasn't the first time."

They bantered for an hour on the right approach with Davis III and the strategy for the defense. "Chris, we have two former co-workers on our witness list who will testify she was a good colleague with no problems, but will they be credible compared to an employer's testimony?"

"Good question; I think the employer will carry more weight. Davis III needs to decide our next steps."

Everything is ready for the morning. Amanda decides she'd like to spend some time on the law library computers. "Chris, I am going to do some research to see if there were any cases in Marshalltown that involved Dr. George Myers. I'd like to access the newspaper database and see what stories about him are in their local paper."

"I'll let you tell me about your findings; I need to wash some clothes. I'll cook dinner for us at the condo. Come over whenever you get tired of stalking your grandfather," he smiles as he waves and leaves.

In the law library, she starts with Marshalltown's newspaper, the *Times-Republican*. She finds many articles about Dr. Myers and his wife at various fund-raisers, social events, and grand openings. She is enjoying the newspapers society section. In a small-town newspaper, you learn who visited whom, who was out eating dinner with whom, who has guests in their home, who's son is going into the service, who's daughter is getting married, and who served tea. I imagine the local newspaper column writers enjoyed receiving calls from friends and neighbors with news and rumors for these columns. Amanda talks to the computer, "I wonder if grandmother, Toni, will submit a story about her long-lost granddaughter coming for tea last Saturday." She chuckles at the thought.

Amanda started scanning the society section in August 1992. She finds one small reference in the third week of August: *MaryAnne Blanc will study abroad this school year.* Amanda finds many pictures and articles about the basketball prowess of young Robert Myers in his junior and senior years of high school. The society page in the summer of 1994 showed: *Robert Myers, son of Dr. and Mrs. George Myers, has accepted a scholarship and will attend the University of Iowa this fall.* Leaving sports and society columns, Amanda does a global search on the newspaper from 1960-1995, keying in a search for: 'Dr. George Myers, Marshalltown, Iowa.' Several thumbprints list the available articles on the left with the newspaper name and dates on the right. Amanda scans the thumbprints and thankfully finds no news about unethical medical behavior or complaints by patients.

She then finds and opens an obituary for Dr. Alan Scott Myers; reading it, she discovers her great-grandfather. He was a lifelong, prominent resident of Marshalltown. He practiced medicine until his retirement in 1974 and owned several commercial and apartment buildings. The obituary lists Robert and Charles as his grandsons. Amanda prints the obituary and congratulates herself; her instincts were right. Her great-grandfather was a doctor.

Three months after his death, an article reports that his son is contesting the estate of Dr. Alan Scott Myers. According to the article, the old Dr. Meyers left his entire estate to his two grandsons, Charles Myers of Marshalltown and Robert Myers of Iowa City. The will filed with the probate court shows Dr. George Myers will inherit only the house he now lives in and the forgiveness of a one hundred thousand dollar loan. The lawyers for Dr. George Myers asked the court to set aside the current will and accept a will dated ten years earlier. Dr. George Myers claims his father lacked the mental capacity to understand the details and implications of the new will signed two years ago. Dr. George Myers further states he was the sole heir in a prior version of his father's will. To further complicate legal matters, Charles Myers, the owner of Myers Certified Public Accountant, LLC and the son of Dr. George Myers, was named as the executor of this extensive estate. A separate newspaper article states Charles Myers filed a petition, asking the courts to remove him as the executor, and requested the court to appoint a qualified lawyer in his place. The court approved Charles Myers' request.

Amanda switches from the newspapers to the legal database. She finds the case in Marshalltown and follows the public documents through the courts. She learns two things. First, it was a waste of time, money, and emotions for Dr. George Myers. The court ruled against him and ordered the distribution of the estate to the grandsons. Second, the amount of money involved in this dispute was shocking. Amanda now understands why Dr. George Myers wanted the courts to accept an older version of his father's will. Her hands shake as she mentally calculates the amount of money the heirs of her birth parent's estate will receive.

Reaching for her phone, she sends a text to Chris, "I'm on my way, see you in a few minutes."

Amanda decides to skip an Uber ride and walks the few blocks up the hill on Grand Avenue to Chris' condo. She calls her mother and uses the time to bring her up-to-date on all that has happened.

Chapter 21

◇◇◇◇◇◇

Over dinner, Brittainy updates Evan, her husband, on her family. "I received a call today from Uncle Charles; he had some amazing news. One of my mother's twins contacted him through Ancestry messaging, and he has met her."

"What's her name?"

"Her name is Amanda Springs, she's twenty-seven years old, and she is an attorney in Des Moines. Last Saturday, she drove to Marshalltown; she and Charles had lunch at the country club and spent the afternoon together. She even met my grandmother. He called because he wants to know if I would like to meet her."

"Did you tell him that you got your DNA results last Friday, and there is an AmandaS on your shared matches?"

"No, I should have, but I was more interested in his news."

"Did he give you her contact information?"

"Yes, he did."

"Before you call her, let's take a look at your DNA matches again. Evan and Brittainy pull up chairs at the computer desk. They study the DNA matches that she has displayed. Pointing at the screen, he says, "OK, here's your mother; she told you a few years ago she was doing a DNA test, and there's your sister, Kayla. And here's your half-sister Amanda Springs, but there's no other half-sister listed. Why isn't her twin listed in the test results?"

"Good question. Evan, look at the top of the list; it's a male with enough centimorgans to be a parent. Oh my God, this match is labeled 'Rwendell,' that's my birth father!"

Evan suggests she click on Wendell's shared matches to see if Amanda is related to him.

"No, she doesn't share DNA with Wendell. So, she is one of my mother's twin daughters with RJ."

"I'm not going to deal with Wendell now; I'm going to call Amanda and introduce myself." Finding the notes from her call with Charles, she dials the number. "Hello, is this Amanda Springs?"

"Yes, it is."

"Amanda, my name is Brittany Myers Evans. I'm your half-sister; we share the same birth mother. My uncle Charles called me today and gave me your telephone number. Is now a good time to visit?"

"Brittainy, I'm glad you called; yes, now is a good time."

"Before we start chatting, Amanda, do you have the FaceTime app or the Zoom app on your cellphone."

"Yes, I have both."

"Would you be willing to do FaceTime video call instead of this voice call? I'd love to see your face as we talk."

"Yes, let's hang up; call me back."

"Ok, see you in a minute."

The cellphone rings, and Amanda accepts the call; Brittany's face appears. She's a beautiful young woman. "Amanda, you look like the pictures of our mother when she was in her late twenties. You also look like RJ."

"Who's RJ?"

"Sorry, that's the name we called your birth father, Robert Myers. He was our adoptive father, and instead of calling him Dad, we started calling him RJ, and it stuck."

"Brittainy, I can see some similarities in our looks. Same hair color, facial structure, even our noses look alike."

Brittany suggests, "you have RJ's eyes."

"I've seen a few pictures of Robert, and I agree. Brittainy, what can you tell me about our mother, and what, if anything, do you know about my twin sister?"

"Let's start with your twin sister. I know she exists; that's about all. My mother told me she gave birth to twin girls when she was sixteen. She told me when I was a teenager, and I think she didn't want me to make the same mistake. I know that somehow they found you about five or six years ago, and before the accident, they hired a private detective to try to find your twin. To my knowledge, the private detective has never located your twin. I know that RJ's estate has been on hold; the will requires a two-year moratorium to allow time to find your twin sister."

"How do you feel about that?"

"Amanda, you cannot imagine how much our mother went through from 1992 until she died in 2019. She and RJ were adamant that their twin daughters, when found, would be part of the distribution of their estate. Even though they'd never met you, you were a big part of their hearts and a member of their family." Amanda sees the tears welling in Brittany's eyes.

"I have wondered about MaryAnne's life. Charles and Toni avoided all conversations about MaryAnne and her parents; I think they felt her story was for you and Kayla to share. Do you have the time and the emotional strength to go into the details tonight?"

"Yes, I'd like to share the story of her life." Brittainy takes a deep breath, "this will take some time to tell. You already know from Charles and grandmother that she got pregnant at sixteen and lived with her aunt in Minnesota. Mom told me that the nurses took you and your sister out of the delivery room moments after you were born; she never saw either of you again. She was heartbroken that she never got to hold you or smell the sweet smell of her newborn babies. She went into a depression and cried for days.

"Before telling their parents about the pregnancy,

she and RJ had decided they would marry; he even bought her a wedding ring with a tiny diamond in it." Brittainy holds up her hand and shows Amanda that she has possession of the ring. "I wear it every day in memory and as a reminder that I can manage life's challenges."

"RJ talked with his grandfather before he garnered the courage to confront his father. His grandfather insisted that he speak with his father. If George were agreeable, he would give RJ a loan and a place to live in one of his apartment complexes. RJ agreed he would work part-time and do whatever was needed to get them through high school and college. They loved each other and knew life would be challenging, but they felt they had enough maturity, commitment, and love to manage a family at their young ages.

"I'm assuming that Charles or grandmother told you it didn't work out as planned. George refused to allow them to marry, brought in the attorney, and no arguing moved him off his position. Mom was sent away, supposedly for a year abroad for schooling. She agreed to go to Minnesota because she didn't want to embarrass her parents. RJ tried for months but could not find her. Ultimately, Dr. George Myers won control, and our mother and your father were separated." She sees Amanda with tears in her eyes, nodding her head that she had heard the story.

"I'll never forget the quiet winter night sitting before the fireplace, Mom was reflecting on her life, or perhaps she wanted me to learn from her mistakes. I just had my first period that day; we spent the day together preparing me for my monthly curse and talking about how babies were born. Like I didn't need her birds and bees story; we'd covered it graphically in sex education classes. But I listened as a good daughter should.

"She told me that she continued to live in Minnesota with her aunt and enrolled to get her GED. She was too embarrassed to return to Marshalltown and face her former classmates. Even though her parents rumored 'she was studying abroad,' her friends all knew the truth. Marshalltown is a small city, and Mom knew the gossip was like a buffalo stampede through the town. Everyone knew the truth; returning to Marshalltown High School to get her diploma was not an option.

"Amanda, I need a break and want to get a glass of wine."

"Great idea, Brittainy; I'll be right back, too." With wine glasses visible on the video call, Amanda says, "Cheers, sister; I'm glad to meet you and hear about our mother."

Brittany continues, "To my knowledge, Mom didn't see or talk with RJ throughout pregnancy or after you girls were born. She didn't have the money to go to college. So, Mom worked as a waitress and then in other menial office jobs as a file clerk. She met her first husband, who, by the way, just showed up on my Ancestry DNA match list as RWendall. He's my birth father; they married just three months after their first date. Mom was lonely; she was starving for affection. Nine months later, I was born, and he wanted her to give me up for adoption. He said he wasn't the nurturing father type, and rich people would pay her a lot of money for her baby. Mom said she was not giving me up regardless of how difficult life would be. She would find a way to survive and manage Wendall's need for her constant praise and attention."

"She sarcastically called him, 'Mr. Wonderful.' He worked at odd jobs, drank most days, and contributed little to the family income. He made enough that they could afford a small apartment with the barest of necessities. He treated Mom poorly, was verbally abusive, and got her pregnant again. Wendall bolted like a jackrabbit when she announced that she was pregnant with Kayla. He left her alone to raise two children, and she never saw him again.

"Mom struggled for the ten years after you were born, both mentally and financially. She was as poor as a church mouse. After her husband left her, we lived again with my great aunt, and she took care of me while Mom was working. She helped Mom a great deal by buying her clothes and giving her money when she was on her last dime. She even helped Mom financially and emotionally with her divorce. My great aunt didn't have any children; I think Mom gave her a purpose in life.

"A couple of years later, Mom got a good job at the local telephone company where they had a daycare center for the children of employees. Life was a little better for her then.

"Charles and grandmother probably told you the story of how RJ and Mom found each other again." Amanda nodded her head that she'd heard the story. "They managed a long-distance relationship, but within six months, they were married, and we all moved to Iowa City. Then everything was amazing, and much joy and love surrounded us. RJ adopted Kayla and me, and we became a real family. I learned from my great aunt that RJ drove to St. Cloud after they were married and personally gave her a huge check to thank her for the care she had given MaryAnne. Mom said her aunt retired the next day." She smiled, "I've always liked that part of the story.

"Amanda, when mother died, I found her diary in the top drawer of her dresser, and I read it. She expressed many of her thoughts, much sorrow, and deep personal disappointments about her life. The birth of the twins, the struggle to survive with two young daughters, and the ten-year separation from RJ all weighed heavily on her mind. I've never shared her most intimate thoughts with anyone, not even my sister, Kayla, but I think you and your sister would appreciate reading her diary. If Mom hadn't died suddenly, I'm sure she would have destroyed her diary so no one would know what she was doing and thinking during those dark days.

"After they married, RJ and Mom had a son, Adam. He's my half-brother and your full brother. I assume again that you heard about Adam from Charles and grandmother."

Amanda nods and holds her hands together, pressing them tightly to her lips. She's trying desperately to control her emotions after hearing the sad story of her mother's life. It wasn't until she was almost my age before life gave her a break and returned Robert into her arms.

"Amanda, RJ was a great Dad and the only father I knew. He adopted Kayla and me within the year after they married. He was a wonderful role model for what I wanted to find in a husband. He loved Mom unconditionally; they were true sweethearts. He supported her desire to get an education and to have a meaningful purpose in life. She loved her work at the University. That's our mother's story; she was a beautiful, loving mother and friend."

Tears flowed on both sides. The two sisters bonded over the story of a woman Amanda never knew and Brittainy can't forget.

Catching her breath, Amanda wiped a tear that lingered on her cheek and said, "Brittany, you are a beautiful person, and your story of our mother brought her to life for me. I am sorry I never got to know her; I now feel her spirit and kind soul. She was conscientious, determined, and loving. Thank you for sharing your memories.

"How is your sister, Kayla," Amanda inquires.

"I talked with her last night. She's been a beach bum in California for a few years. I think she has come to terms with the loss and has found herself. She says she's coming back to Iowa, but her plans change faster than the speed of light. I won't believe it until I see the whites of her eyes." She laughs for the first time.

"One last question, what about MaryAnne's parents?"

"As you can imagine, they were devastated when their only daughter became pregnant; sending her away was one of the hardest things they'd ever done. Giving Dr. George Myers control over the adoption of their twin granddaughters was one of their biggest regrets. Grandpa Jon worked for the Lennox Corporation as a maintenance supervisor. When Lennox moved their headquarters to Dallas, Texas, they offered Grandpa a transfer. He jumped at the chance, wanting to get out of Marshalltown and away from the memories. Grandma Gabriella was less enthusiastic; she didn't like the idea of being 750 miles away from her daughter and granddaughters, but they both learned to love Texas and the warmer climate. Grandpa's retired now, and they are busy with their church and hobbies. I still see them twice each year, once in the summer and then at Christmas. I hope you want to meet them; I know they would be thrilled to meet you. They will be elated when they hear that I've met and talked with one of the twins."

Amanda smiles, knowing that her grandparents are still living and enjoying life. When she finds her twin, a trip to Texas will be high on her priority list.

Chapter 22

◇◇◇◇◇◇

Amanda realized she had turned her cell phone off last night after her lengthy conversation with Brittainy. Turning it on, it exploded with text messages from Jennifer. "Amanda, call me." "Amanda, where are you? I have news." The last message announced triumphantly, "Amanda, I've found your twin sister."

Amanda looked at Chris across the breakfast table with a massive smile on her face. Her hands were shaking as she turned her cell phone towards him so he could read Jennifer's new message. "Amanda, this is great news; call her."

Amanda dialed quickly, reaching the wrong number; she apologized for the inconvenience. She tries a second time, but her fingers again misdial. Handing the phone to Chris with a look in her eyes that says 'please, help me,' he takes her phone and dials the correct number. She asks him to put it on speakerphone—she wants him to share the moment.

"Jennifer, this is Amanda. I'm sorry I turned my phone off last night after a long conversation with my half-sister, Brittainy. Your text messages are sensational and breathtaking. I can't believe you've found my twin sister. Where is she?"

"She's in Missouri. If you check your 23andMe account, you will find that you have a new match with a nephew. He is not a half-nephew but a full nephew. Based on your family tree, the only person that could have given birth to a full nephew is your twin sister. I don't know why her son submitted a genetic DNA test, but I'm glad he did.

"I found an obituary in Cross Corners, Missouri for Garrett Tanner, whose wife's name is Tiffany Tanner. The obituary lists Isaac as a son, so I know I have the right family. Also listed is a daughter, Melissa Tanner." Jennifer pauses and then continues, "Amanda, I'm ninety-nine percent sure that Tiffany Tanner is your twin sister. She's living in northwest Missouri, about a two or three-hour drive from you. As much as I would like to call to confirm what I know to be true, I know it's your journey and not mine. Please get in touch with her. Her telephone number and other contact information are in the email I sent you."

Speechless, Amanda is thrilled by the news and elated to have finally found her twin. Chris says nothing but comes close, gives her a big hug, provides a reassuring hand and a warm smile.

"Jennifer, thank you. You are truly my Angel. I can't believe you found her."

"Amanda, please call me and let me know what happens. Half the reason I volunteer with Search Angels is I enjoy the search and building family trees for adoptees. The true enjoyment is hearing how my work has affected them. Please, please let me know what happens." She assures her that she will not forget her Angel's request.

Before hanging up, Amanda shares with Jennifer what she has learned from Charles and Brittainy; all the pieces are falling into place. "Talk with you soon, Jennifer. Bye for now."

She sits smiling at Chris. "This is like Christmas in July. I like that you were with me when I received this present. Finding Emma is wonderful news. Who do I call first? My parents? Tom Graves? Charles—"

Chris interrupts, "Just a suggestion, Amanda, but why don't you call your twin sister first?" He smiles at her, and she smiles back, somewhat embarrassed.

"What happened to the cool, collected attorney," she thinks to herself. "Get a grip," she chastises herself.

She opens her email box and finds Jennifer's message, and hands the phone to Chris. "Please, my fingers don't seem to work today. Would you dial the number for this incredible call of my life?"

The phone rings five, six, and then seven times; she must not be home. Suddenly, a familiar voice–a voice just like mine—says, "Hello."

"Is this Tiffany Tanner?"

"Yes, it is."

"Tiffany, my name is Amanda Springs, I thought I knew how to handle this call, but now I seem unable to put two coherent words together." She pauses for several seconds, collecting her thoughts before continuing, With a strangled voice, "Tiffany, is your birthdate March 3, 1993?"

"Yes, it is. Why do you ask?"

"I believe you and I are twin sisters separated at birth and adopted into separate families."

No response, dead silence. Finally, some words, "Why do you think that?"

Amanda carefully chooses her words, "Well, I know that I was born on March 3, 1993, and my twin sister was born two minutes after me. I have had a personal conversation with my biological grandmother, who was there at my birth and confirms twin girls were born. The Springs family adopted me, and my twin, Emma, was adopted by another family through the Des Moines Social Services. We were born in St. Cloud, Minnesota." She pauses, listening to Tiffany's quick breathes and perhaps tears. "Tiffany, I have a genetic genealogist working with me, and she is certain that you are my sister."

It seemed like an eternity before she responded. "I don't know what to say at this moment; you've caught me quite by surprise. My birthdate is March 3, 1993, and my middle name is Emma. I'd like to process what you're suggesting and call you back. Would that be okay?"

"Yes, yes, of course. Tiffany, I was able to find you only because your son submitted a DNA test to 23andMe. He showed up in my matches as a nephew. My twin sister is the only one in my family tree that could have produced a nephew. Take your time, process your thoughts, check your son's 23andMe account, and look for a matched labeled AmandaS; that's me. Call me when you're ready. Do you have my number on your caller-ID?"

"Yes, I do."

"I'll eagerly await your return call. Tiffany, no pressure, but I have much to share with you when you're ready."

A tiny insecure voice responds, "Thank you for calling. I'm sorry for my hesitancy. I am not aware that I was adopted, nor have I ever heard anything about a twin. I need to have a conversation with my parents. I will call you soon." The line went dead.

"I feel bad; she didn't know she was adopted. I should have anticipated that. She lost her husband a year ago, and now I've upset her life and put her into a tailspin."

Amanda quickly sends a text message to Charles, Brittany, and Tom Graves "Twin sister found. Emma, now Tiffany Emma Tanner, lives in Cross Corners, Missouri."

Amanda's cell phone rings. She quickly grabs it and checks the caller-ID; the number is foreign to her. She turns to Chris. "Looks like another spam call. Let's have some fun. Whatever they want to sell me, I'm

A DNA Adventure

going to insist on more information about my car insurance warranty, which are the most annoying spam calls I receive." Chuckling to herself, she answers the phone, "Hello."

She's surprised when the caller asks, "Is this Amanda Springs?" She acknowledges they have the right person. "Amanda, my name is Michael Matheson; you and I have a DNA match on Ancestry.com.

"Yes, Michael, I've seen the match and received your message. Nice to finally talk with you. So, how do two strangers who are related start this conversation?"

"Let me give it a try. I was shocked, no, stunned—" there's a long pause, "I guess damn angry to learn that the father who raised me is not my birth father. Then to realize I have two half-brothers and a half-niece that I'd never met was just the icing on the cake."

"Michael, I could say 'Ditto,' but my surprise was not only you but two half-sisters, a full brother, an uncle, and a twin sister. Just to let you know, I'm a great gal, and I haven't embarrassed you in the last two decades of your life." She responds with a chuckle in her voice. "It's been quite a journey for me, but with your call, all the pieces have fallen into place."

With a smile in his voice, Michael says, "I like your attitude. My brother, Matt, is the family genealogist. He'd exhausted his search through paper records and decided DNA would be a new great adventure. Well, it was for him, but not so much for me."

"Well, it's your lucky day; you've found a great relative and a happy one. Tell me about yourself."

"Happy to do so, but I would like to share with you what I've learned in the last several weeks and see if you have any other tidbits of information to add to my story." He shares his DNA results, his conversation with his mother, her confession about infertility issues, and her denial of any sexual relationship with any other man.

"Michael, did your mother live in central Iowa about the time of your conception?"

"Yes, she and my dad were students at Iowa State University."

"Did she perhaps tell you that her doctor helped her with infertility issues?"

"Yes, what is it you know that I don't?"

"Michael, your mother is telling you the truth. There was a well-liked and successful fertility doctor who lived in Marshalltown, Iowa. Marshalltown is just 30 minutes east of Iowa State; he helped women become pregnant. He had the husband bring in a sperm sample, claiming he would apply additives to boost the sperm. After injecting the sperm via intrauterine insemination, the women generally conceived. Unfortunately, it wasn't a *boost* to the husband's sperm but a replacement with someone else's sperm. In your mother's case, she received the sperm of my grandfather. That's how we became related."

"What! How sick is that?"

Amanda pauses before responding, "Yes, I agree, Michael. I've just learned some of the facts, and it's a long, complicated story; who was the doctor in your mother's life?"

"Not a clue," he replies.

"Michael, hug your mother and let her know she didn't do anything wrong. As tragic as it is, she was just taken advantage of by a doctor who considered himself God. He's dead now; in fact, he's been gone several years, and his last years on this earth were not pleasant ones."

"So, Michael, you are my half-uncle, and I'm happy to welcome you to my crazy family. Unlike you, I was adopted at birth, have great adoptive parents, and have a wonderful life. I knew as a little girl that my parents weren't my biological parents. But I never knew until a few weeks ago that I have a twin sister and all these other relatives. On a scale of one to ten, I trump you on being stunned."

"OK, you win the prize for the most surprised. But it's still a kick in the head for me."

"I agree. It has been stressful, but I'm now coming to terms with all the relationships. As shocking as it has been, it has also been a pretty cool experience. I met my Uncle this last weekend. He still lives in Marshalltown and is a nice, responsible guy and a successful CPA. I even met my grandmother; she's still living in the old family home. Now when I say grandmother, don't think of an older woman with gray hair. Think about a woman who looks sixty, wears leggings and fashionable modern clothes. She is more active than many people in our age demographics."

"I'd love to meet you at some point, but for now, I think I'll close the chapter on this DNA business. Thanks for the information; it explains a great deal. It's water over the damn, and we can't change the past. Mother will be relieved that I've learned the truth, and we can put this saga behind us."

"Michael, thanks for calling. Enjoy every day, and we only get to go round once in this life."

Amanda turns to Chris, "that was my half-uncle, Michael, in Seattle. He sounds like a nice guy. I didn't give him any names, but if he thinks about it, he can probably figure out who all the players are in the drama of his birth."

A text message pings on her cell phone, "Amanda, call me when it's convenient. Charles Myers."

"This is a busy night for phone calls from my new family members." She dials his number. "Hello, Charles, I was just talking about you."

"Really, why?"

"I just had my first conversation with Michael in Seattle, and I was sharing that I just met you."

"I assume you shared the sperm donation project. How did he react?"

"Quite well. Michael had already had a conversation with his mother and knew she didn't have sexual relations with another man. She admitted she went to a fertility specialist, so one plus one equals two. I don't think he likes that a doctor took advantage of his mother, but I think he understands that his family has nothing to gain by making a fuss about it now that your father is deceased. By the way, he never asked, and I never offered the name of the doctor involved. I don't expect that he will join in any of our family activities; I think he's just going to get on with his life."

"I sent you a text message because I have news. I talked with Adam, and he's more than excited to meet his big sister. He says that his parents told him about the twins when he was thirteen; he's excited that DNA helped locate you. Brittainy sent a text saying she had already had a FaceTime conversation with you. She thinks she's going to like having you as a sister. The big news is Kayla; she's coming back to Iowa. She, too, wants to meet you. I can't thank you enough; you're bringing our family back together. The grief has caused all of us to be lost, each in different ways. The return of the lost twins and your enthusiasm is giving all of us a new focus."

"I don't know what I've done to deserve your thanks, but you're welcome."

"I got your text; you've found your twin sister. How did that happen?" Charles quietly asks.

"Yes, I have," Amanda explains how Jennifer made the connections and shared her conversation with Tiffany. "I contacted the Des Moines Social Services, and I'm waiting for them to call back. They are checking their adoption records for an Emma born on March 3, 1993. Now I don't need the information, but Emma may be interested in learning what's in her file."

"I couldn't be happier for you; I'm only sorry my

brother and his wife didn't have the chance to meet you. But the other family members are eager to do so, and Mother wants you to come to Marshalltown for Labor Day if you're available. Yes, I know it's a long way off, but she's an organizer and plans well in advance. She has front row seats to the Marshalltown fireworks and would like you and Chris, and now Tiffany, to join the family for our annual picnic celebration. If you'd like a place to stay, you are welcome to stay at our Marshalltown home."

"Please, thank your mother for the invitation; I will check with Chris and get back to you. Thanks for the overnight offer, but I know Chris would be more comfortable in a hotel."

"Will Brittainy and Adam be there for Labor Day?"

"Yes, and with luck, Kayla will be back from California. I'll be watching for your message and hope you can join us." Amanda clicks to end the call and stares at her phone.

Chapter 23

◇◇◇◇◇◇◇

Her office door opens, and Chris sticks his head in, "You ready to go? Lark Monahan just arrived for his deposition. Davis III's assistant called with a five-minute warning; we are meeting in the executive conference room upstairs."

Grabbing her file and notes, she smiles and says, "No worries, I'm ready; just been sitting here waiting." She quickly crosses to the door, bringing her smile from her face up to her eyes as she confidently joins him on the walk up the staircase.

The deposition went as expected; no surprises. He hired Darla to be his bookkeeper because his business was growing, and he needed someone with experience to handle the bookkeeping. He did check the references she provided before offering her the job. He liked her talents and her experience as a watchdog on expenses. After the first year, he even entrusted her with his non-business checkbook to pay his personal bills. Then he started hearing from his vendors that their invoices were not being paid regularly or on time; he always prided himself on promptly paying all bills. He visited with his certified public accountant when he found a letter from General Motors stating that their parts invoices were in arrears. The following day, the CPA firm conducted an unscheduled audit.

The CPA discovered several cashed checks were missing in the files. The bank provided copies; all had been made payable to and cashed by Darla Wilson. In response to several questions, he replied:

"No, I had no deal with her to share a percentage of anything she saved him.

"No, there was no concern about General Motors; he paid the delinquent bills immediately.

"Yes, Darla saved the dealership about fifteen thousand dollars by verifying that all employee reimbursements and vendor invoices were complete and accurately submitted.

"Yes, I discussed my concerns about the late payment of vendor invoices on her last performance review.

"Yes, I reported the theft of $97,000 to the police after the CPA's completed his audit and discovered the many checks were written to and cashed by Darla."

The deposition of Lark's certified public accountant followed. The CPA confirmed that several cashed checks were missing in the files and that the bank provided copies of the check images. He assured us all checks had been made payable to and cashed by Darla Wilson. All of the amounts on the checks matched a dollar amount on an invoice for one of Lark's vendors. According to the CPA, the dealership printed checks using an old sprocket-fed check-writing machine. Darla was manipulating the print ribbon as she issued checks to the vendors. Therefore, the original copy of the check was blank, but the carbon copy showed a payment to a vendor. The carbon copy showed the vendor's name, the amount paid, and the carbon copy would be attached to the vendor's invoice and then filed. The check, however, was issued with her name in the 'pay to the order of' line. They all agreed the CPA would be a credible witness for the prosecution team.

The subsequent meeting with Davis III went equally well. He understood the difficulties of defending the case and knew he would have a considerable challenge at the defense table. He appreciated our work and will give our recommendations careful thought. He agreed to get back with a direction on how to proceed and what additional research was needed. The judge has set the case for trial in three weeks.

The entire day sped swiftly by like a fast-moving train. Amanda and Chris felt chained to their desks all day. The client appointments and telephone calls never ceased. The best call of the day was from her Rotary colleagues; they had selected her to be the attorney for their new business. Her marketing plans worked. She had secured her first new clients for the firm.

The phone rings, "Is this Amanda Springs?"

"Yes, it is. Who's calling?"

"This is Des Moines Social Services. You inquired earlier this week on your adoption through our agency in 1993." Amanda ignores that it wasn't her adoption but her twin sisters. "I'm sorry, but there is no information on the location of your twin sister. There are, however, two letters added to the file six years ago by your birth parents; one for you and another for your twin. I can send you a copy of the letter written to you."

"Can you scan the document and send it to my email? I'd like to see it today, if possible."

"No worries, I'll have it on its way in the next fifteen minutes." She thanked her for her call and help. "When you find your twin, please let her know there's a letter waiting for her, too."

When she'd made the last client call, Amanda grabbed her purse and walked to Chris' office, which was uncharacteristically dark. He must have left early. She secures a place on the full elevator and heads home; she feels somewhat lonely without Chris by her side.

As she opened the door to her loft, her cell phone started ringing. "Amanda, are you home?"

"I just walked in the door; I missed you. You weren't in your office when I left. Where are you?"

"I'm just leaving my condo. I was hoping you could put on your walking shoes and meet me at the Pappajohn Sculpture Park. I'm headed there, now."

"I'll leave in a minute and see you there."

"Meet me by Gary Hume's sculpture of the *White and Black Snowmen*. Let's enjoy this beautiful weather. We can appreciate the art, and then I'll take you to DJango for dinner."

"Aren't you concerned that we might run into one of the partners, either at the park or at the restaurant?"

He paused for a moment, then chuckled, "No, not tonight; the partners are at the Des Moines Art Center gala fundraiser. Didn't you get the memo?"

"You're a funny guy Mr. Reed. Are you picking up the dinner tab tonight?" she jokingly inquires.

"My treat. See you in fifteen minutes." She quickly changes into a vividly colored sundress. One glance in the mirror, she grabs her purse and heads down the elevator.

Walking the five short blocks to the park, she passes many brown metal planters; they look like upside-down pyramids set atop an open weave pedestal. They give the street an air of artistic beauty; the colorful flowers and cascading green vines make her feel happy as she leans closer to breathe in the fragrance. Amanda smiles and sighs with pleasure; she loves living in the heart of the city.

Arriving at the park, she follows the sidewalk around the grassy mound and sees Chris by the *Black Snowman*. She feels butterflies in her stomach at seeing him and enjoys the warmth that moves through her body at the sight of her handsome man. He gives her a whistle of approval as the wind whips her skirt above her knees. "You look stunning in that dress." She rushes forward to give him a grateful hug for his compliment. He kisses her briefly and starts walking toward the next fantastic art sculpture. "Did you know this four-and-a-half acre park has more than forty million dollars invested in large sculptures, each created by a world-renowned artist?"

"You should be a tour guide or part of the Chamber of Commerce. You love this place," she comments.

Standing in front of the red two-story *LOVE* block letters, Chris pauses to read the artist's name, Robert Indiana. He wants to remember all the details of this moment. He turns toward Amanda with soft, inviting eyes, "Have I told you that I love you?"

She smiles broadly, "Not today."

He kisses her passionately, and he pulls out his cellphone to take a selfie in front of the artwork. He sees debris on the sculpture and kneels to remove it. Turning toward Amanda and resting on one knee, he opens a box extending it toward her. The jewelry box contains a brilliant two-carat cut diamond.

At first, she doesn't realize what's happening. "Oh my God, are you doing what I think you're doing?"

"Yes, Amanda, I am. I love you; I've known since the first day I looked into your beautiful eyes that I wanted to be with you for the rest of my life. Will you marry me?"

He removes the ring, stands upright, and with a questioning, hopeful look and a raised eyebrow, he silently asks her the same question.

"Yes, Chris, yes, yes, and yes. I love you, too." He

slips the ring on her finger, pulls her into a tight embrace, and locks a passionate kiss on her lips while allowing his hands to roam.

Suddenly horns from passing cars are honking, and shouts of 'get a room' sink into his brain. He released Amanda and smiled broadly. Touching his forehead to hers, he breathlessly says, "I can't believe you'll be mine."

The euphoric feeling continues as they walk across the park to Juame Plensa's monumental white steel lattice sculpture. It is made of alphabet letters and artistically represented a crouching human shape called *Nomade*. The artwork is hollow in the center, and they walk inside to look through the open latticework. Amanda points to individual letters, spelling out 'I love you.'

She smiles and explains, "When you come in here, you are encouraged to close your eyes and listen to the sounds of the city." She closes her eyes, "All I hear is the wind whistling through the letters."

He smiles at her, "I only hear my heart rapidly beating." They take another selfie, and Amanda turns and looks deeply into his eyes.

"Before tonight, this was my favorite piece of art; now I have to say it's the *LOVE* sculpture."

Crossing the street to DJango, Amanda and Chris hold hands and imagine the future together that is about to unfold.

"Amanda, do you have any plans this weekend?"

"No, what do you have in mind?"

"I want you to meet my parents." They agree to discuss the logistics for the trip later in the week.

As they are seated, Amanda's cellphone alerts her to an email message. She checks the screen and recognizes the sender of the message. "Chris, before I left the office, I got a call from Des Moines Social Services. I inquired on Monday if there was a record of Emma's adoption, and they found her file. Emma has never made contact with them to inquire about her adoption. The adoptive parents have a 'no contact order' on file that dates back to 1993. The exciting news is there were two letters left in the file by our birth parents about six years ago, one for each twin. They just sent me a copy of my letter."

She smiles broadly with excitement in her eyes. "Let's save it for later when we are at the loft and have some privacy."

"Again, you have such willpower; I would be scrolling through the message now."

"I want to share it with you, and this restaurant isn't private enough."

The waiter served their food, and as always, dinner was fabulous. The DJango manager, Gary, is a friend and stops by with greetings. He noticed the ring on Amanda's finger and immediately signaled for a bottle of champagne to celebrate. As they wait for the bottle's arrival, Amanda shares the romantic nature of Chris' proposal in the park. Nearby dining guests pause as Gary makes a production of pouring the bubbly into three flutes. He offers a glass to Amanda and Chris and secures the third for himself. Sweeping his arm wide, he announces their engagement to the nearby dining guests and executes his toast.

"Congratulations," echo throughout the room in response to Gary's eloquent toast.

Tonight is a night of love and romance. They slowly savor their dessert and talk non-stop about their life, their feelings for each other, when and where they'd like to be married, how they will tell their parents, and what their living arrangements should be now and in the future. Amanda feels euphoric and doesn't want this special evening to end.

Leaving the restaurant, they walk east toward Amanda's loft. They briefly stopped by her apartment to grab a bottle of wine, two glasses and headed up the elevator to the rooftop garden. The stars above are bright despite the lights of the city buildings; nothing detracts them from the pleasure of knowing that their life together is just beginning. Time passed like the blink of an eye, and it was time to retire for the evening.

Amanda slips her hand in Chris' as they head to the elevator. Opening the door at the loft, she reaches for the light switch, but Chris stills her hand. Walking backward with a gleam in his eye, Chris leads Amanda to her bedroom. Without breaking eye contact, they slowly undress. Gently, Chris pulls Amanda onto the bed. He cradles her head and slowly kisses her. Amanda hadn't realized she'd been holding her breath. Tonight is a night to remember, and she was going to savor each moment. She rolls Chris over and slowly begins nuzzling his neck and chest. Closing her eyes to enjoy the moment, she feels the urgency building in both of their bodies. Slowly, she straddles Chris, taking his warmth deep inside her. Euphorically, she rocks back and forth until she feels her release approaching. As she splendors in the spiraling sensation, she feels Chris find his release. With tears shimmering in her eyes, she looks down at Chris and whispers, "Thank you for choosing me."

Chapter 24

◇◇◇◇◇◇

The alarm goes off at six a.m. Amanda is startled awake. She always wakes before the alarm—but not this morning. Stretching like a cat, she raises her arms high above her body and arches her back with pleasure. Her eyes catch the sunlight glistening off her beautiful diamond ring, sending splashes of light onto the wall and the ceiling. A dazzling array of lights dot the room. Rolling over, she finds Chris still sleeping soundly. With a five o'clock shadow and messy hair, he looks terrific. She can hardly believe she will wake each morning for the rest of her life with this handsome man at her side.

She snuggles in closer. Chris stirs, stretches, and gives her a big smile, "Good morning, beautiful," he says, reaching for her hand and kissing her ring finger. Checking his watch and realizing the time, he starts extricating himself from the bedcovers. "I have to head to my condo and clean up for the day." He leans over Amand to give her a slow and longing kiss. He throws on last night's clothes and then stops in his tracks. "Amanda, we forgot about the letter from your birth parents; did you open it last night?"

Amanda stares at him like a deer stuck in the headlights of a car. "In the excitement of last night, I forgot all about it. I'll save it for tonight, and we can experience it together. Go clean up; I'll see you at the office."

"Amanda, it can't be that long of a letter. Are you sure you don't want to read it now, before launching into Hell and the legal world?" She chuckles at his humor. She grabs her iPad from the nightstand and clicks on her email message. Bringing up the attachment, she agrees—it's not long.

Amanda catches her breath, "Chris, the Des Moines Social Services thinks I'm my twin sister; they've sent me her letter."

"Mistakes happen; enjoy it."

Amanda begins reading the letter out loud:

Dear Emma,

We are your birth parents and have been looking for you. We've gone to great lengths to learn who adopted you and have a private detective looking for you. You will be eighteen years old this year (2011). We have loved you since the day you were born, and we hope you find this letter waiting for you at your place of adoption.

If you are holding this letter in your hand, please

call us at 319-252-7355 or ring the doorbell at our home in Iowa City, Iowa at 2745 University Avenue East. We are waiting to hear from you and will welcome you back into our lives. Your birth father is Robert Myers, and your birth mother is MaryAnne (Blanc) Myers. We were teenagers in high school when we fell in love and created you. Our parents, understandably, felt they knew the appropriate future for you and took control to give you a better life. At my ten-year class reunion, we found each other again, married, and are now raising our family. You have a twin sister, Amanda Emily Springs, who will graduate from Pella High School in Pella, Iowa. The terms of her private adoption do not allow us to approach her, but we've both put our DNA on Ancestry.com and 23andMe in hopes that you and she will initiate contact with us. Emma, please know that we never wanted to give you or your twin sister up for adoption. There were circumstances beyond our control. We will tell you about our love and life and answer any of your questions when we have the blessed opportunity to see you. We've thought about you every day since 1993, and we hope to find you and get to know you. With love from your birth parents, God bless you wherever you are.

Robert and MaryAnne (Blanc) Myers

The tears well in Amanda's eyes, and she finds it challenging to finish the last words of the letter. Chris pulls her into his arms and gives her a warm, comforting hug. "Amanda, your parents, were trapped by their youth, but they were warm, caring people. Your sister will love to receive this letter when you see her. I can't wait to see what they wrote to you." The tears stream from Amanda's eyes, but she has a smile on her face.

"Go, go get ready for work. I'll cry in the shower and see you at the office. I love that my birth parents sound warm, sensitive, and loving. I'm sorry I didn't get to meet them, but I have a brother and two sisters who knew them well."

Chris gives her a hug and heads out the door for a quick jog to his Grand Avenue condo. He thinks along the way that he needs to consolidate some clothing to her loft and eliminate these early morning dashes back to his place. Life is changing, and he likes the direction.

It was an exciting day at the office; she added another new client and spent the morning doing initial research on their legal issues. The telephone never stopped ringing, and billable hours came quickly.

At noon she met Justice Sandra Calhoun for lunch at Cafe Barattas, a rooftop cafeteria in the State Historical Museum of Iowa. Amanda shared how much she liked her job in Hell's business litigation department, her boss, and most of all, Chris. She extends her hand, drawing attention to her ring finger. Justice Calhoun smiles broadly. She's delighted that Amanda has found the love of her life. "What about the search for your birth parents, anything new?" For the next thirty minutes, Amanda shared the results of her journey, meeting her uncle and grandmother and now finding Tiffany. It was an exhilarating lunch, and she knew the justice would be a mentor for years to come. She's thankful for the support and interest.

That evening she and Chris are at his condo having dinner talking excitedly about the day when Amanda's cell phone rings. She notices the caller-ID number is from Missouri. "Chris, it's Tiffany!"

"Tiffany, hello, I've been waiting for your return call."

"Amanda, I'm sorry I was unable to deal with our telephone conversation last week. I've talked with my parents and learned that they had adopted me as a newborn, just as you stated. It explains why I'm an only child. My parents were sorry that they'd never told me, but there never seemed to be a right time. As time passed, they were embarrassed that they hadn't said something earlier and then decided I may never learn the truth. They decided not to disturb my life. But, Amanda, they didn't know that I had a twin; they are just as surprised as we are."

"Tiffany, are you available next weekend? I want to drive to Missouri and meet you. I have much to share with you, and I have a letter addressed to you from our birth parents. I can come around eleven and spend the day; if that works for you."

"Yes, please come on Saturday. We live on a farm. I'll send you a text message with directions."

"Tiffany, I'm excited and eager to meet you. Since we are identical twins, I have visions that we might feel like we are looking in a mirror. I know when I hear your voice over the phone, it sounds like me talking to myself. Sorry, I'm rambling. Thank you for calling tonight. See you soon. Good night."

Chapter 25

◇◇◇◇◇◇

Turning off Interstate 35 to the west, Amanda had an immediate wake-up call. Coming over the top of the hill, she was startled to see a slow-moving farm tractor towing a large piece of farm equipment. It was taking up the entire road, and she had no way to get around it. She hit the brakes quickly to avoid a collision. The farmer pulls over at the next intersection to allow her to pass. Lesson learned, she carefully maneuvers her car through the winding, undulating green hills of Northwest Missouri. It's almost ten forty-five on a gloriously sunny summer day. She's looking for Cross Corners, a small community of primarily farmers and farm implement dealers.

Amanda stares out the front windshield and says to herself, "This town is small in size, but it's a big important destination for me and you, Tiffany Emma Tanner."

Amanda is lost in her thoughts when suddenly there's the sign, Cross Corner, Missouri, population fifteen hundred, just one mile more. Amanda is feeling both anxious and excited. In less than ten minutes, she will pull into a farm driveway and meet Tiffany, the person with whom she spent the first nine months of her life.

Amanda finds the driveway to the Tanner farm; it's a beautiful entrance with white picket fences lining each side from the road to the house. Soybeans are growing on the right; on the left is a field of corn that is knee-high. She remembers the adage that the corn yield would be good if it's 'knee-high by the fourth of July.' She wonders if corn farmers still believe that to be true.

Driving in slowly, she sees Tiffany and two children coming out of the white, wood-framed two-story farmhouse. Beyond the house stands the typical red barn, the equipment sheds, and a small yellow house. Everything is immaculate and tidy, just like a Norman Rockwell painting. Two blue Harvestore silos stand like sentries beside the barn. From conversations with her dad, she knows that they are the premium silos for fodder. That means the Tanners must feed livestock or dairy cows. However, she doesn't see any sign of animals other than the collie winding through the children's legs.

As she approaches, Tiffany is waiting on the side of the driveway. She's dressed in a pretty sundress with her hair tied back in a casual ponytail and smiles as

Amanda steps out of the car. With a big smile on her face, her twin stretches out her arms, inviting a welcoming hug. "Wow, Amanda, you are right; I feel like I'm looking in a mirror. How did you know we were identical twins?"

Amanda returns the smile and laughs. "When I had tea with our birth grandmother, she shared our birth story."

Tiffany has called the local paper, and Amanda sees a man off to the side snapping pictures. The kids are patiently standing behind their mother, waiting for an introduction. "Amanda, these are my children. Meet my daughter, Melissa; she's eight, and my son, Isaac; he's seven."

"It's nice to meet you both; I'm your Aunt Amanda."

Isaac looks from his mother to me and back again, "Mommy, why does she look just like you? What's an Aunt?" The sisters both laugh out loud. Tiffany ruffles the hair on top of his head and promises to explain it all later. She has, obviously, not shared the news with them yet.

The local newspaper photographer captures the moment of Isaac looking up somewhat bewildered at his mother and his aunt. Amanda can mentally see the headlines already. A story with pictures of twenty-seven-year-old twin sisters meeting for the first time would be big news in a small town. She turns to the photographer and asks if he would share his picture and story with the *Pella Chronicle*. He agrees to notify her hometown paper. As they slowly walk to the farmhouse, the photographer takes one final photo and heads for his pickup truck.

They enter the kitchen with enormous smiles and find an older man and a younger woman seated at the kitchen table. Coffee and coffee cakes are waiting on the Formica table. "Amanda, I'd like you to meet Ted Tanner; he's my father-in-law and lives in the yellow house on the back of the property."

Ted stands to greet her, "You've certainly brought some excitement to our household. It's a pleasure to meet you."

"And, this beautiful woman is my neighbor, my best friend, Marlene, who lives on the farm just east of here." Instinctively she raises her arms and points in the direction of Marlene's farm.

Marlene is full of excitement. "I was astonished when Tiffany told me about being adopted and having a twin sister, and I can't get over how much you look alike. You could switch places, and no one would ever know."

Amanda chuckles, "Like in the movies? I don't think I could pull it off; I know nothing about running a farm."

Marlene smiles broadly with a friendly welcome expression in her eyes. "I'd sure like to be a little mouse in the corner today to hear the stories you'll share, but it's not my place." She invites us to have fun as she turns and whisks the children out the door; they will stay with her for the afternoon.

"I'm out the door, too," says Ted Tanner, "the work on this farm doesn't get done without me. I'll leave you be; if you need anything, give me a holler, I'll be out back in the equipment shed." With a smile on his face and a squeeze on Tiffany's shoulder, he heads out the door.

Finally, they are alone, surrounded by Tiffany's old-fashioned, unpretentiously designed farm kitchen with lots and lots of counter surfaces. The appliances are sturdy. The heavy iron gas range has six gas burners, and the finish is white enamel with black specks. The dishwasher is the kind on wheels. When it's time to wash dishes, someone has to roll the dishwasher to the sink and connect the hoses to the faucet. When the cleaning cycle is complete, the appliance returns to the end of the counter, where the dishes are allowed to dry. Not quite as convenient as the modern built-in appliances, but it works.

The expanded open kitchen is where the family lives; a TV area is on the right with oversized comfortable chairs and a sofa. There's a large wooden table in the corner with white bentwood chairs surrounding it. This area is for kids' activities; crayons, paints, and paper cover the top of the table.

A huge eight-foot-long window above the farm-style sink bathes this room with warm sunlight. Antique open-face shelves and a wood-beamed ceiling finish off the charming look and make the area inviting. Amanda sighs at how peaceful she feels here. "Tiffany, this room is marvelous; it's large but still comfortable and cozy. My entire loft would fit in this kitchen." she laughs.

"Thank you. My husband designed and remodeled this kitchen so the family could all be in one room together. It's my favorite spot in the house. Amanda, I am eager to know how you found me."

"Jennifer, my Search Angel is the one to be credited."

"Your what?"

"When you have a chance, go on the internet and do a computer search on Search Angels, you can read about this organization. They are volunteers who help adoptees find their birth parents through DNA test results.

"Your son is only seven years old, so he's not old enough to order a test kit. But it was his DNA results and the obituary about your husband, Garrett, that finally made the connection that allowed me to find you. Tiffany, I am sorry you lost your husband, and your children lost their father; he was incredibly young. It must still be difficult for you all" Tiffany says nothing, lowers her eyes to her lap, and shakes her head affirmatively, "May I ask why you had Isaac take the test?"

"I ordered the test kit for both Melissa and Isaac because I have been out of my mind with worry about Garrett's cancer. I am worried that his cancer might genetically pass to my children. Marlene told me about 23andMe. I checked it out on the internet and found that it generates reports related to one's ancestry and genetic predispositions for health-related issues. I insisted the children spit in the vial. I'm sure you'll see Melissa's DNA match soon. I'm a little worried that I possibly have exposed my children to identity theft or that my health insurance company could inappropriately use their DNA results."

"Tiffany, I understand your concerns. I'm sorry cancer caused you to test your son and daughter, but I am happy you did. If your children's test results keep you awake at night, you can always delete the DNA results and their 23andMe accounts."

"Tiffany, when I called you, you didn't know you were adopted. I'm sorry, I should have anticipated that as a possibility. It never crossed my mind that you wouldn't know."

"No, I didn't know. My parents never told me, and now that I've confronted them, they are embarrassed. They wonder why they kept it a secret. They are nice people, but I never looked like them. When I would ask, they would say I looked more like my grandmother, who died before I was born. I didn't have any siblings, my mother wasn't able to have children, but they were loving people, always involved in the community, especially the church. Being an only child on a farm is lonely; no one to play with; my dolls became my best friends as a young girl; I can't tell you how many weddings I had for Ken and Barbie." She chuckles. "Garret, my husband, was an only child, so you can understand why Isaac asked, 'what's an aunt?'"

"I've known since I was able to read a book that I

was adopted. The children's books my parents gave me were frequently about little girls who were 'selected' by their parents through adoption. It was never unsettling for me; they were just my parents."

"Amanda, your unexpected news is truly welcome. I like the idea that you were in the world as my sister, even if circumstances did not allow us to be together. But I would have loved growing up with you by my side."

"Well, I didn't know I had a twin until just a few weeks ago. You were my surprise. I contacted the social services agency where you were adopted." She hands her the letter from their birth parents. "Somehow, I must have unintentionally given them the impression that I was the twin adopted through their agency. They send me a copy of this letter meant for you." Amanda waits and watches as Tiffany reads the letter addressed to Emma. They smile at each other with eyes glistening with welling tears. "When you come to Des Moines, we'll have to go back to the agency; there's a letter waiting there for me, too.

"Let me tell you what I've learned about our birth parents, Robert Myers and MaryAnne Blanc." For the next two hours, Amanda shares her parents' high school romance, the birth of twin girls in St. Cloud, Minnesota, the parent's death in a sudden car accident, and everything revealed by the DNA tests. She shares information about each of the newly discovered uncles, a brother, and half-sisters.

Tiffany, an only child, is amazed that she now has

so many siblings; she's not sure how to process all of this new information. "Have you met them all?"

Amanda shakes her head, "No, I've only met Uncle Charles and our grandmother in person and Brittainy on a FaceTime call. But now that I have found you, I'd like to meet everyone. We can do it together, but it will be a challenge; the family lives across the country: Seattle, California, Missouri, Wisconsin, Texas, and Iowa. Grandmother has invited us to join the annual Myers Labor Day family picnic in Marshalltown. Mark your calendar, and I'll get more details as we get closer to the date. You'll want to bring your children and your father-in-law to this family reunion." Amanda shares more about her adoptive family, her work, and her recent engagement with Chris.

"He sounds wonderful, Amanda." Tiffany reciprocates by sharing her high school romance and marriage to Garrett Tanner, their children, their life on the farm, his death from cancer, and her loving father-in-law. She regrets that she didn't go to college, but she and Garrett were in love. Tiffany shared that she and Garrett had started a savings plan for their children's college educations; they both need to get a college degree. But her other worry is the stress from the financial challenges of running the farm. The land is worth a fortune, but the yearly costs of operations have been a drain on their savings. She loves the farm and knows her son and daughter will inherit the property when Ted passes. She's sad that her father-in-law's plans for retirement were interrupted.

Before his death, Garrett was carrying the load, and now all that has changed.

Amanda shares her final surprise, her luncheon meeting with Tom Graves. She explains they have to meet him in Iowa City before the end of the year. The closing of their birth parent's estate has been held open pending the location of the twin daughters. They will both benefit from an unexpected inheritance from their birth parents. Amanda explains that they will learn the details of the will when they meet with Tom Graves. Tiffany is speechless and pinches herself to be sure all of this is real.

Amanda and Tiffany share pictures of their early childhood lives and laugh at the same *geeky* looks they had in junior high school. They try to cram a lifetime into one afternoon but agree they will need to schedule some weekend time to get to know each other. Amanda hands Tiffinay the two photo albums of their father in high school and college. She shares the scrapbook that Charles gave her and explains how Robert found the pictures and articles. "Charles gave them to me with instructions to share them with you. It looks like you have more bookcases and storage than my little loft; I'll leave them in your safe care."

As the early evening arrives, Amanda regrets that it is time to leave; she needs to get back to Des Moines. She agrees to return soon and asks if she can bring Chris. Goodbye hugs and kisses occur before Amanda gets into the driver's seat and buckles in for the ride back to Des Moines. Amanda rolls down the window with one parting thought, "Tiffany, next time, I'd like to get to know my niece and nephew." A huge smile appears on Tiffany's face as she says goodbye to Amanda. She waves as her sister drives down the long farm driveway on her way back to her city life.

As she stands in the driveway watching the car disappear, Tiffany quietly says, "Thank you for coming into my life, sister."

Amanda calls Chris. He answers promptly, "Hey, girlfriend are you on your way home?"

"Yes, I'm just leaving Tiffany's; I have much to tell you. We had a great day together; she looks exactly like me. I can't wait until you meet her. I promised to return, and I hope you will join me; she's eager to meet her future brother-in-law. She is a beautiful person inside and out."

"Well, you two have that in common. What time will you get home?"

"Probably not until eight-thirty."

"Come to my condo. I will chill a bottle of champagne, and we will go down by the pool to relax and celebrate your success in finding your sister. Spend the night, and I'll take you to Louie's Wine Dive for breakfast."

"I'd like that, Chris; I'll see you in a couple of hours."

Chapter 26

◇◇◇◇◇◇◇

The telephone rings. "Tiffany, it's Amanda, I'm sorry to call this early, but I just got off the telephone with our birth parent's attorney, Tom Graves. He needs a DNA test from each of us to confirm that we are, in fact, twin sisters of Adam. Wait until he sees us together; he will be blown away by how identical we are, but physical looks do not make it in a court of law. He's already sent DNA test kits to us via one-day delivery; we should receive them this morning. He needs us to spit in the vial and ship them back by the end of the day. Mailing labels and instructions for the return will be in the package. He has a lab at the University Hospitals standing by to expedite the test results. Do you have access to Fed-Ex or UPS near you?"

"Yes, the local variety store handles the one and two-day delivery of packages for Cross Corners. I'll watch for the truck to arrive and will return it today."

"Tom is thrilled that we've found each other, and he wants to arrange a meeting with all the heirs to the estate. He's hoping to have our DNA results by this Friday and would like to schedule a meeting in Iowa City for the following Friday morning. He needs us to be present in his office because he has several documents we need to sign."

"Will you drive over for the meeting on Friday morning, Amanda?"

"No, I plan to go over on Thursday afternoon; I'd like to see if we could have dinner with Charles and meet our brother, Adam."

"If I drove to Des Moines Thursday morning, could we drive together to Iowa City?"

"Tiffany, that sounds like a plan. I'll let Tom know that we will both be in his office a week from Friday. I'll make reservations at a local Iowa City hotel and call Charles."

"Amanda, do you know who else will be at this meeting?"

"I don't. But if it's a reading of the will, I would expect all heirs to the estate will be there. So, our brother, Adam, Uncle Charles, his legal guardian, and possibly via video conference, Brittany who lives in Wisconsin, and Kayla who lives in California."

What about our half-uncle, Michael?" Tiffany inquires.

"He wasn't even known to Bob and MaryAnne. There's no way he will be an heir. I'm excited to meet everyone." Tiffany shares the same sentiment.

"Tiffany, on the drive over, I'd like to discuss a fun idea. As Marlene suggested, there have been many comedy movies where twins switch places. Tom Graves has met me; let's see if he can tell the difference." Amanda chuckles with the thought of duplicity. "I'll explain my idea on the drive over."

"Amanda sounds to me like you have a fun, devious streak in your make-up; I like that. It was part of my personality before I lost Garrett. I need to find that fun side of life again. I'll see if Dad and Marlene can watch the kids next week. I'll plan to arrive around eleven on Thursday morning. On the return, I'll stay in Des Moines Friday night and return to Missouri on Saturday."

"Tiffany, don't get a motel room; you can stay at my place on Friday night; I'll stay with Chris. I'd like to have you meet Chris; we'll find a place for dinner, and I think champagne will be in order."

"Amanda, I can't tell you how surreal all of this is to me. I can't believe I have a twin sister and that I'm driving to talk with an attorney about being an heir to an estate. Things like this don't happen to a little farm girl from Missouri. If I lived in Kansas, I would think I was Dorothy from the *Wizard of Oz*." They both chuckled.

"I know it's been quite a journey for me, and you're just getting on this ride. Ok, text me when you've sent in your test kit; I'll do the same. See you in eleven days."

Amanda hangs up the phone, sits back in her office

chair, and stares out the window. Whispering to herself, she exclaims, "Wow! What a journey! Tiffany is warm and inviting; I know we are going to have a good time getting to know each other." She makes a mental note to call her mother and bring her up-to-date on all that has happened.

Chapter 27

◇◇◇◇◇◇◇

Her assistant opens the door, "Amanda, Davis III's office just called. He would like to see you and Chris in his office in fifteen minutes."

"Thanks, Lisa. Does Chris know?" Amanda looks at her engagement ring and wonders.

"Yes, he does."

Ten minutes later, she's out the door, taps on Chris' window, and they march together up the sweeping staircase. "Got any idea what he wants today?"

"No, we'll just have to wait and see."

Entering the office, Davis III greets them with a warm, inviting smile. "Let's have a seat on the comfortable sofa and chairs. I want to give you an update on the Darla Wilson case. After Lark's deposition and your debriefing on the status of the case, I met with Darla and her father. I explained the difficulties in the defense; I assured them that we were ready for trial, but there were no guarantees what the jury would believe. I explained the prosecutor's witness list and the evidence that a former employer would present, and the evidence will show that this wasn't her first financial problem with an employer. They understand that Darla's demeanor in the courtroom and her creditability as a witness could win or lose the case. J. Gifford and Darla were left alone in the conference room to discuss how they wanted us to proceed. In the end, J. Gifford agreed to reimburse Lark Chevrolet for the $97,000, which Darla will repay to her father over time, probably many years. Darla will plead *no contest* to the charge if the Polk County Attorney agrees to full restitution and probation instead of jail time. I visited with the Polk County Attorney, and we've negotiated an acceptable outcome for both sides. The trial will not go forward. I want to thank you both for your time and efforts on this case; you've done an excellent job."

"Great work on your negotiations, sir. I think this is the best outcome for all concerned," Chris states. Davis III stands to indicate the meeting is over. Amanda and Chris head toward the door.

"One more thing," Davis III smiles, "Congratulations, I hear there's a wedding in your future." He turns without further words and walks to his desk as Amanda and Chris exit the office.

As the door closes, Amanda and Chris high-five. "Congratulations, counselor," Amanda says in celebration.

Chapter 28

◇◇◇◇◇◇

Thursday arrives; it's eleven, and Tiffany is at the security desk when Amanda steps of the elevator and greets her with a big hug. "Come up to my office and meet Chris."

Tiffany is more than impressed with the Ruan Center and Amanda's work environment. "You work here?" asks Tiffany. "I'm intimidated by these surroundings; everything is impressive, and you can just feel power and prestige seeping out of the walls."

"Don't be too impressed; I'm just a new attorney expected to produce incredible billable hours. Let's have some fun with Chris. We'll stand at his door; I'll hide my hand and ring behind my back. Then you say, "Chris, I'd like you to meet my twin sister. I know he will do a double-take and for a brief moment wonder who's who."

They walk down the hall toward her office and

stop at Chris' door. He quickly rises from his chair and stops dead in his tracks. Tiffany pulls off her lines, and Chris' head bobbles back and forth, first looking at one and then the other. He walks confidently over to them with a gleam in his eye. Grabbing Tiffany, he bends her back in his arms as though he's the 1945 WWII sailor on V-J Day in New York's Times Square. As he raises her back up without having kissed her, he looks into her eyes and says, "Tiffany, it's nice to meet you." They burst out laughing. "You are hilarious girls, but I know who's who. And Amanda, I've been with you all morning; I'm observant, and I don't think you switched clothes coming up the elevator," he smiles triumphantly.

He extends his hand in a proper greeting. "Tiffany, I'm Chris. I can't tell you what a pleasure it is to meet you." Tiffany stops and stares. She's a little stunned by his theatrics and, also, impressed with the looks of her handsome future brother-in-law.

"Tiffany, Chris has been on this journey with me since day one. He has supported me through all the DNA results, including the ups and downs of my adventure."

"You two do look identical; it's amazing. You should wear name tags tomorrow when you meet Tom Graves."

"I agree," says Amanda. "I have a plan." She draws out two name tags from her purse; both say 'Amanda Springs.' "We'll have a little fun tomorrow and see if he knows which one is the Amanda Springs he had lunch with a couple of months ago. By the way, Tiffany, Tom sent me a text today; he has the DNA results, proving we are twin sisters and that we are the big sisters of Adam."

"Chris, we are off to Iowa City. Want to walk us to the car?" she smiles and winks. They head down the elevator, and she gives him a hug and a warm, gentle kiss. "Didn't think we should say goodbye in the office." She smiles. "I'll call you tonight and again after we meet with Tom. See you for dinner around five-thirty tomorrow at the 801 Chophouse." She smiles at him and silently mouths, "*I love you.*"

"Drive carefully."

Arriving at the Hilton Garden Inn near Tom's office, Tiffany and Amanda quickly unpack and freshen up. They are meeting Charles and Adam for dinner at the Vue Rooftop restaurant of their hotel. When the elevator door opens, they are mesmerized by the 360-degree view of Iowa City. Amanda approaches the hostess stand and inquires about a reservation for Myers.

"Yes, the other guests have already arrived; follow me, please." She guides them to a large black leather booth that provides some privacy for this special evening. As they approach, they see three other people seated with Charles.

He rises and approaches Tiffany and Amanda, "There is no doubt that you are twins. I would give you a hug, Amanda, and say nice to see you again, but frankly, I don't know who is who."

They chuckle at Charles' confusion. "I'm Amanda," she steps forward and gives Charles a warm hug "nice to see you again." Stepping back to include her sister in the family circle, "This is my sister, Tiffany Emma Tanner."

Charles takes her hand in both of his and plants a kiss on each cheek. "Your parents looked for you for several years, and we still have a private detective on retainer. It was your smart sister and her genetic genealogist that made this all possible."

"Well, maybe it is our parents we should thank," chimes in Amanda. "They are the ones that put their DNA out for discovery and sent a lawyer to have lunch with me."

"Yes, maybe so. I'm sorry that your birth parents can't be here to meet you; I feel that they are here in spirit and pleased about this reunion. Let me make some introductions." Everyone is standing, and a circle of the six family members forms. "This is my wife, Sherry; she's the strength in this family. She held us all together in the darkest days of 2019." Tiffany and then Amanda reach toward her for a welcoming hug. "This is Adam, your brother."

He's not a hugger but gives each of them a high-five with a wide grin from ear to ear. "Nice to meet you both. I've heard about the twins," he does air quotes with his fingers, "for the last four or five years. I feel I already know you. Mom told me the story about being separated from you at the time of your birth and how it made her feel sad. Like Uncle Charles, I wish they could have been here to meet you; it was their dream to find you."

Charles continues with the introductions, "Amanda, you've already met Brittainy."

"Yes, I have, but it's nice to see you in person." They reach for each other for a tight hug. "Brittainy, meet our sister, Tiffany."

As she walks toward Tiffany, she extends her hand and then pulls her in for a hug. The smile on Tiffany's face lit up the room, and the tears in her eyes glistened.

"I have one more introduction. From around the corner, a gorgeous tall girl dressed in tight jeans and looking like a fashion model comes out of the kitchen area and approaches those gathered. The noise erupts as Brittainy and Adam swarm the girl with hugs, kisses, and broad laughing smiles. She lifts her brother in her arms and turns him in a circle; the joy on their faces shows their love and affection for each other. Amanda and Tiffany couldn't help but smile and enjoy the love shared by this family.

Charles hugs Kayla and turns her toward the twins "Amanda and Tiffany, this is your sister, Kayla. She flew in today from California." With sheer joy on their faces, all five siblings step in for a simultaneous group hug.

"What a welcome this has been," says Tiffany.

A waiter with a tray of champagne approaches the table and offers everyone a glass of the bubbly. Charles grabs a second glass and hands it to Adam. He wants him to share in the toast. Raising his glass, Charles offers, "After all that has happened, I can only quote the last words of Czar Alexander I of Russia: *"What a beautiful day."*

To secure a second sip of the champagne, Adam offers a toast. "Here's a toast and blessing that all your hopes and dreams come true."

Charles and Sherry look at each other with surprise on their faces. Taking a sip of the champagne to honor his toast, Charles turns to Adam, "Where did you hear that toast?"

"I just made it up; I wanted another taste of this forbidden fruit." As Charles lifts the glass out of Adam's hand and pours the contents into his own, they all laugh.

The evening flew by; several conversations were going on simultaneously. Everyone seemed comfortable and interested in each other's life stories and memories. After eating dinner, they lingered around the table and seemed to play musical chairs; everyone wanted an opportunity to talk with the twins and with Kayla.

Amanda and Tiffany returned to their hotel room, exhausted from interaction, laughter, and family stories. Amanda sighed, "What a wonderful night."

Amanda leaves Tiffany in the hotel room and goes down to the lobby to call Chris. She shared her observations with Chris and her feelings about the evening. He laughs as she explains Adams clever toast to get another sip of champagne.

"That would be something I would have done, clever young man." Finishing her call, she says good night and heads back to the room. Tiffany is already sound asleep on one of the queen size beds.

Morning arrives too quickly. They both shower and dress, then head to the dining room for a light breakfast. Promptly at ten o'clock, they arrive at Tom's office; they are escorted to his conference room by the receptionist.

The family members, excluding Charles' wife, Sherry, are already seated and waiting for Tom. Hugs all around as the twins join them. The six family members continue where they left off last night with more laughter and joyful conversation. *I forgot to tell you last night* was a common phrase used by everyone around the room.

Tom walks into the room and smiles at the family gathering. Amanda and Tiffany had strategically placed themselves near the door. As he approached them, they both turned to face him. Tiffany extends her hand, "Tom, nice to see you again."

He sees their name tags, both saying Amanda Springs, and starts laughing. "I saw the DNA results, and you are identical twins, but honestly, I don't know which one of you is the real Amanda."

Tiffany takes off the name tag, "Mr. Graves, I'm Tiffany Emma Tanner; it's a pleasure to meet you." Everyone in the room chuckles at their little gag.

Tom opens his briefcase and spreads five sets of documents on the table. Amanda extends her hand to

Tiffany's arm, "Don't be intimidated by this show of paperwork; it's how we lawyers gather attention."

Tom Grave chuckles, "She's right, but in this situation, all these documents are incredibly vital to you."

"First, Tiffany, I can't tell you how happy I am to meet you. I am only sorry that my friends, your birth parents, didn't have the same opportunity. They had been looking for you for several years before the accident. Unfortunately, your whereabouts were still unknown when they were suddenly and sadly taken from this earth. Nonetheless, they made provisions in their will for all five of their children, with instructions that their estate would remain open for two years after their death to give adequate time to find Emma."

"Here are the terms of their will. He distributed five copies, one copy for each. Tom explains that Charles has liquidated all the estate's remaining assets except for the house on University and the personal property therein. All the debts, including the remaining mortgage on the home, have been paid. Charles has paid the taxes for the estate, and he filed all taxes, as required. The only expenses remaining to the estate are the current legal fees and the cost of closing the case in court."

Amanda quickly follows along easily as Tom reads the legal language in the will and the various requirements for the distribution to the heirs. In summary, Adam can live in the house until he graduates from college. Charles will continue as his guardian until Adam is twenty-one, and he will manage a fund to take care of the house and Adam's expenses. The remaining value of the estate will be distributed to the heirs today. Charles will sell the house within the next ten years, and the proceeds will be distributed equally among the five children.

Amanda remembers Chris' question: *what happens if your twin is still unlocated by the deadline.* Now she knows. The terms of the will stipulate that the executor would hold Emma's share in a trust fund until the sale of the house. That would have allowed another ten years to locate Emma.

Tom smiles, rises, and moves slowly down the conference table, placing a packet in front of the four legal adults and Charles as Adam's guardian. "It is a great pleasure to have all five heirs of Robert and MaryAnne (Blanc) Myers here today. I need your signatures on these documents; it confirms you understand what I have just explained to you. You will each receive the initial distribution of $1.4 million."

Four of the five heirs sucked all the oxygen out of the room. They are overwhelmed by the value of their parent's estate. Only Charles and Amanda anticipated the estate's total value. Thanks to great-grandfather Alan Scott Myers, they are now millionaires with the freedom to change their lives.

Tom coughs and gains their attention. He again rises. "Charles has been the executor for the estate, and he has opened investment accounts for each of you." Tom hands the four sisters their investment account documents. Tom continues, "The money has already been distributed. I suggest you visit your local investment broker, your lawyer, and your tax accountant. When you are ready, you can transfer the funds. Since you are not yet of legal age, Adam, your Uncle Charles, will handle your investments until your twenty-first birthday. I need each of you to sign acknowledging receipt of your portion of the estate. After you've signed, you are free to leave." He places a folder and pen before each person, giving Adam's folder to Charles. They begin reading the documents and signing for their inheritance. Amanda assured Tiffany with each signature that all was legally in order. Tiffany appreciated the expertise of her twin; this was way over her comfort level and knowledge.

Then the tears start to flow relentlessly. Tiffany is overwhelmed by what she has just heard and is speechless beyond belief. Never in her wildest dreams did she expect to gain a sister and find financial independence within the same month. God has truly blessed her. Her children's college education has weighed heavily on her heart and mind. And getting a college degree for herself felt out of reach; until now. An unexpected and fantastic gift arrived on her doorstep this month. She looks at Amanda and her newfound brother and sisters with tears streaming down her face. With tears, all the sisters wrap their arms around Tiffany and share in her happiness and theirs.

Only Adam sits there looking at Charles. "Do you

suppose I could buy a car next year when I turn sixteen?" All the girls are laughing and crying at the same time at his request.

Charles replies, "We'll see what next year brings. OK, my family, let's go to lunch. Sherry is waiting for us at the University Club."

Epilogue

◇◇◇◇◇◇◇

Amanda cuddles next to Chris, feeling secure with her head on his chest. "Chris, I think it's time to give up my loft, sell your condo, and find a place that we can call home. What do you think?"

Eyes closed and nearly asleep, Chris agrees to her plan, "okay, let's start looking next weekend."

With a smile on her face and knowing Chris has not forgotten they are meeting her parents on Saturday, she responds, "OK, but not until after we've had dinner with my parents. Maybe the following weekend would be better."

"I'd like us to consider a long-range plan of opening a new law firm named Reed & Reed Attorneys at Law after we have more experience with Helling, Newbiggin, and Sloan." No reply; she looks over— he's dozed off.

Bells and whistles on the iPad announce a text message. Reaching for it on the nightstand, Amanda reads the text from Jennifer. "Amanda, check your Ancestry account. You have a new half-uncle."

Acknowledgments

◇◇◇◇◇◇◇

To the love of my life and husband of forty-two years, Loy Brooks, thank you for your daily question: "Do you have a new chapter for me yet?" I would not have finished writing let alone, published *Amanda's Journey*, without his support.

To the adoptees—you know who you are—who shared their journeys and allowed me to use my experience to search for their birth parents and families. Your extraordinary stories stimulated the desire to write a book. *Amanda's Journey* is a book of fiction; it does not contain any adoptee's individual story.

A thank you to my golfing friends in Sun City Grand, who encouraged me to write about my journey with the adoptees. To Dyan Griswold, who handed me her notepad and helped brainstorm some initial ideas while we golfed. To Bob Near, Toni Jaskowick, Jo Sloan, Sherry Baehr, and others: readers, contributors, and editors of the early manuscript. To Carolyn Drake and Missy Newbiggin, who over the years helped keep my passion for genealogy alive by making genealogical trips to the Family Search Library in Salt Lake City.

To Mark Dupaul and Lori Conser at Wheatmark, Inc- Book Publishing Specialists, Tucson, Arizona. Many thanks for your advice, education, and creativity. You made the process easy for this first-time author.

Genealogists could not help adoptees find their birth parents without the development of the consumer-direct DNA testing kits provided by AncestryDNA® of Ancestry Publishing, 23andMe, and others. Thanks to these companies for their products and excellent service.

Amanda's Journey
Book Club Review Questions

◇◇◇◇◇◇◇

1. In the first chapter, Amanda introduces the readers to an Iowa sculpture called *Shattering Silence*. What silences did characters shatter, and who revealed the untold stories?

2. Discuss people you've known who were adopted, adoptive parents, or birth parents. What feelings, emotions, or stories did they share?

3. In your life experience, did you know any young girls who got pregnant out of wedlock? What was the attitude of the family and society toward the birth mother? What lifestyle changes were made by the family to avoid the embarrassment of a pregnant daughter?

4. Put yourself in Amanda's life; if you were adopted, would you pursue finding your birth parents? Why or why not?

5. What did you learn about DNA testing from the story? Have you submitted a test? If so, what motivated you to *spit in the vial*, and what did your test results reveal?

6. What are the three major themes or separate stories carried throughout the book? What purpose does each serve in Amanda's journey?

7. What did Amanda learn on her visit with her Uncle Charles in Marshalltown, Iowa?

8. Which character other than Amanda captured your attention? Discuss why you like this character and what they contributed to the story.

9. How did you feel about the ending of the story? Discuss the final sentence in the Epilogue, how is it feasible that she has another half-Uncle. If you were Amanda, would you delete your DNA test results?

About the Author

Ellie Brooks and her husband, Loy, are retired and live in Surprise, Arizona, and Des Moines, Iowa. For more than forty years, Ellie has been a genealogist and has included DNA as one of her search tools for the last six years. When Covid-19 struck the country, Ellie needed a project to fill her time. She decided to use her skills to help adoptees find their birth parents. It became her passion. She was amazed at the stories she discovered and shared with her adoptee clients. *Amanda's Journey* is her first novel.

Made in the USA
Las Vegas, NV
31 March 2022